W9-CGK-463

What Moves
the Dead

TOR BOOKS BY T. KINGFISHER

Nettle & Bone

What Moves the Dead

T. KINGFISHER

What Moves the Dead

NIGHTFIRE

A Tom Doherty Associates Book
New York

This is a work of fiction. All of the characters, organizations, and events portrayed in this novella are either products of the author's imagination or are used fictitiously.

WHAT MOVES THE DEAD

Copyright © 2022 by Ursula Vernon

All rights reserved.

Endpaper art by Ursula Vernon

A Nightfire Book
Published by Tom Doherty Associates
120 Broadway
New York, NY 10271

tornightfire.com

Nightfire™ is a trademark of Macmillan Publishing Group, LLC.

The Library of Congress Cataloging-in-Publication Data is available upon request.

ISBN 978-1-250-83075-3 (hardcover)
ISBN 978-1-250-83078-4 (ebook)

Our books may be purchased in bulk for promotional, educational, or business use. Please contact your local bookseller or the Macmillan Corporate and Premium Sales Department at 1-800-221-7945, extension 5442, or by email at MacmillanSpecialMarkets@macmillan.com.

First Edition: 2022

Printed in the United States of America

0 9 8 7 6 5 4 3 2 1

This one's for the Dorsai Irregulars,
who would make Easton feel right at home.
Shai Dorsai!

What Moves the Dead

CHAPTER 1

The mushroom's gills were the deep-red color of severed muscle, the almost-violet shade that contrasts so dreadfully with the pale pink of viscera. I had seen it any number of times in dead deer and dying soldiers, but it startled me to see it here.

Perhaps it would not have been so unsettling if the mushrooms had not looked so much like flesh. The caps were clammy, swollen beige, puffed up against the dark-red gills. They grew out of the gaps in the stones of the tarn like tumors growing from diseased skin. I had a strong urge to step back from them, and an even stronger urge to poke them with a stick.

I felt vaguely guilty about pausing in my trip to dismount and look at mushrooms, but I was tired. More importantly, my horse was tired. Madeline's letter had taken over a week to reach me, and no matter how urgently worded it had been, five minutes more or less would not matter.

Hob, my horse, was grateful for the rest, but seemed

annoyed by the surroundings. He looked at the grass and then up at me, indicating that this was not the quality to which he was accustomed.

"You could have a drink," I said. "A small one, perhaps."

We both looked into the water of the tarn. It lay dark and very still, reflecting the grotesque mushrooms and the limp gray sedges along the edge of the shore. It could have been five feet deep or fifty-five.

"Perhaps not," I said. I found that I didn't have much urge to drink the water either.

Hob sighed in the manner of horses who find the world not to their liking and gazed off into the distance.

I looked across the tarn to the house and sighed myself.

It was not a promising sight. It was an old gloomy manor house in the old gloomy style, a stone monstrosity that the richest man in Europe would be hard-pressed to keep up. One wing had collapsed into a pile of stone and jutting rafters. Madeline lived there with her twin brother, Roderick Usher, who was nothing like the richest man in Europe. Even by Ruravia's small, rather backward standards, the Ushers were genteelly impoverished. By the standards of the rest of Europe's nobility, they were as poor as church mice, and the house showed it.

There were no gardens that I could see. I could smell a faint sweetness in the air, probably from something flowering in the grass, but it wasn't enough to dispel the sense of gloom.

"I shouldn't touch that if I were you," called a voice behind me.

I turned. Hob lifted his head, found the visitor as disappointing as the grass and the tarn, and dropped it again.

She was, as my mother would say, "a woman of a certain

age." In this case, that age was about sixty. She was wearing men's boots and a tweed riding habit that may have predated the manor.

She was tall and broad and had a gigantic hat that made her even taller and broader. She was carrying a notebook and a large leather knapsack.

"Pardon?" I said.

"The mushroom," she said, stopping in front of me. Her accent was British but not London—somewhere off in the countryside, perhaps. "The mushroom, young . . ." Her gaze swept down, touched the military pins on my jacket collar, and I saw a flash of recognition across her face: *Aha!*

No, *recognition* is the wrong term. *Classification,* rather. I waited to see if she would cut the conversation short or carry on.

"I shouldn't touch it if I were you, officer," she said again, pointing to the mushroom.

I looked down at the stick in my hand, as if it belonged to someone else. "Ah—no? Are they poisonous?"

She had a rubbery, mobile face. Her lips pursed together dramatically. "They're stinking redgills. *A. foetida,* not to be confused with *A. foetidissima*—but that's not likely in this part of the world, is it?"

"No?" I guessed.

"No. The *foetidissima* are found in Africa. This one is endemic to this part of Europe. They aren't poisonous, exactly, but—well—"

She put out her hand. I set my stick in it, bemused. Clearly a naturalist. The feeling of being classified made more sense now. I had been categorized, placed into the correct clade, and the proper courtesies could now be deployed, while we went on to more critical matters like mushroom taxonomy.

"I suggest you hold your horse," she said. "And perhaps your nose." Reaching into her knapsack, she fished out a handkerchief, held it to her nose, and then flicked the stinking redgill mushroom with the very end of the stick.

It was a very light tap indeed, but the mushroom's cap immediately bruised the same visceral red-violet as the gills. A moment later, we were struck by an indescribable smell—rotting flesh with a tongue-coating glaze of spoiled milk and, rather horribly, an undertone of fresh-baked bread. It wiped out any sweetness to the air and made my stomach lurch.

Hob snorted and yanked at his reins. I didn't blame him. "Gahh!"

"That was a little one," said the woman of a certain age. "And not fully ripe yet, thank heavens. The big ones will knock your socks off and curl your hair." She set the stick down, keeping the handkerchief over her mouth with her free hand. "Hence the 'stinking' part of the common name. The 'redgill,' I trust, is self-explanatory."

"Vile!" I said, holding my arm over my face. "Are you a mycologist, then?"

I could not see her mouth through the handkerchief, but her eyebrows were wry. "An amateur only, I fear, as supposedly befits my sex."

She bit off each word, and we shared a look of wary understanding. England has no sworn soldiers, I am told, and even if it had, she might have chosen a different way. It was none of my business, as I was none of hers. We all make our own way in the world, or don't. Still, I could guess at the shape of some of the obstacles she had faced.

"Professionally, I am an illustrator," she said crisply. "But the study of fungi has intrigued me all my life."

"And it brought you here?"

"Ah!" She gestured with the handkerchief. "I do not know what you know of fungi, but this place is extraordinary! So many unusual forms! I have found boletes that previously were unknown outside of Italy, and one *Amanita* that appears to be entirely new. When I have finished my drawings, amateur or no, the Mycology Society will have no choice but to recognize it."

"And what will you call it?" I asked. I am delighted by obscure passions, no matter how unusual. During the war, I was once holed up in a shepherd's cottage, listening for the enemy to come up the hillside, when the shepherd launched into an impassioned diatribe on the finer points of sheep breeding that rivaled any sermon I have ever heard in my life. By the end, I was nodding along and willing to launch a crusade against all weak, overbred flocks, prone to scours and fly-strike, crowding out the honest sheep of the world.

"Maggots!" he'd said, shaking his finger at me. "Maggots 'n piss in t' flaps o' they hides!"

I think of him often.

"I shall call it *A. potteri*," said my new acquaintance, who fortunately did not know where my thoughts were trending. "I am Eugenia Potter, and I shall have my name writ in the books of the Mycology Society one way or another."

"I believe that you shall," I said gravely. "I am Alex Easton." I bowed.

She nodded. A lesser spirit might have been embarrassed to have blurted her passions aloud in such a fashion, but clearly Miss Potter was beyond such weaknesses—or perhaps she simply assumed that anyone would recognize the importance of leaving one's mark in the annals of mycology.

"These stinking redgills," I said, "they are not new to science?"

She shook her head. "Described years ago," she said. "From this very stretch of countryside, I believe, or one near to it. The Ushers were great supporters of the arts long ago, and one commissioned a botanical work. Mostly of *flowers*"—her contempt was a glorious thing to hear—"but a few mushrooms as well. And even a botanist could not overlook *A. foetida*. I fear that I cannot tell you its common name in Gallacian, though."

"It may not have one." If you have never met a Gallacian, the first thing you must know is that Gallacia is home to a stubborn, proud, fierce people who are also absolutely piss-poor warriors. My ancestors roamed Europe, picking fights and having the tar beaten out of them by virtually every other people they ran across. They finally settled in Gallacia, which is near Moldavia and even smaller. Presumably they settled there because nobody else wanted it. The Ottoman Empire didn't even bother to make us a vassal state, if that tells you anything. It's cold and poor and if you don't die from falling in a hole or starving to death, a wolf eats you. The one thing going for it is that we aren't invaded often, or at least we weren't, until the previous war.

In the course of all that wandering around losing fights, we developed our own language, Gallacian. I am told it is worse than Finnish, which is impressive. Every time we lost a fight, we made off with a few more loan words from our enemies. The upshot of all of this is that the Gallacian language is intensely idiosyncratic. (We have seven sets of pronouns, for example, one of which is for inanimate objects and one of which is used only for God. It's probably a miracle that we don't have one just for mushrooms.)

Miss Potter nodded. "That is the Usher house on the other side of the tarn, if you were curious."

"Indeed," I said, "it is where I am headed. Madeline Usher was a friend of my youth."

"Oh," said Miss Potter, sounding hesitant for the first time. She looked away. "I have heard she is very ill. I am sorry."

"It has been a number of years," I said, instinctively touching the pocket with Madeline's letter tucked into it.

"Perhaps it is not so bad as they say," she said, in what was undoubtedly meant to be a jollying tone. "You know how bad news grows in villages. Sneeze at noon and by sundown the gravedigger will be taking your measurements."

"We can but hope." I looked down again into the tarn. A faint wind stirred up ripples, which lapped at the edges. As we watched, a stone dropped from somewhere on the house and plummeted into the water. Even the splash seemed muted.

Eugenia Potter shook herself. "Well, I have sketching to do. Good luck to you, Officer Easton."

"And to you, Miss Potter. I shall look forward to word of your *Amanitas*."

Her lips twitched. "If not the *Amanitas,* I have great hopes for some of these boletes." She waved to me and strode out across the field, leaving silver boot prints in the damp grass.

I led Hob back to the road, which skirted the edge of the lake. It was a joyless scene, even with the end of the journey in sight. There were more of the pale sedges and a few dead trees, too gray and decayed for me to identify. (Miss Potter presumably knew what they were, although I would never ask her to lower herself to identifying mere vegetation.) Mosses coated the edges of the stones and more of the stinking redgills pushed up in obscene little lumps. The house squatted over it like the largest mushroom of them all.

My tinnitus chose that moment to strike, a high-pitched

whine ringing through my ears and drowning out even the soft lapping of the tarn. I stopped and waited for it to pass. It's not dangerous, but sometimes my balance becomes a trifle questionable, and I had no desire to stumble into the lake. Hob is used to this and waited with the stoic air of a martyr undergoing torture.

Sadly, while my ears sorted themselves out, I had nothing to look at but the building. God, but it was a depressing scene.

It is a cliché to say that a building's windows look like eyes because humans will find faces in anything and of course the windows would be the eyes. The house of Usher had dozens of eyes, so either it was a great many faces lined up together or it was the face of some creature belonging to a different order of life—a spider, perhaps, with rows of eyes along its head.

I'm not, for the most part, an imaginative soul. Put me in the most haunted house in Europe for a night, and I shall sleep soundly and wake in the morning with a good appetite. I lack any psychic sensitivities whatsoever. Animals like me, but I occasionally think they must find me frustrating, as they stare and twitch at unknown spirits and I say inane things like "Who's a good fellow, then?" and "Does kitty want a treat?" (Look, if you don't make a fool of yourself over animals, at least in private, you aren't to be trusted. That was one of my father's maxims, and it's never failed me yet.)

Given that lack of imagination, perhaps you will forgive me when I say that the whole place felt like a hangover.

What was it about the house and the tarn that was so depressing? Battlefields are grim, of course, but no one questions why. This was just another gloomy lake, with a gloomy house and some gloomy plants. It shouldn't have affected my spirits so strongly.

Granted, the plants all looked dead or dying. Granted, the windows of the house stared down like eye sockets in a row of skulls, yes, but so what? Actual rows of skulls wouldn't affect me so strongly. I knew a collector in Paris . . . well, never mind the details. He was the gentlest of souls, though he did collect rather odd things. But he used to put festive hats on his skulls depending on the season, and they all looked rather jolly.

Usher's house was going to require more than festive hats. I mounted Hob and urged him into a trot, the sooner to get to the house and put the scene behind me.

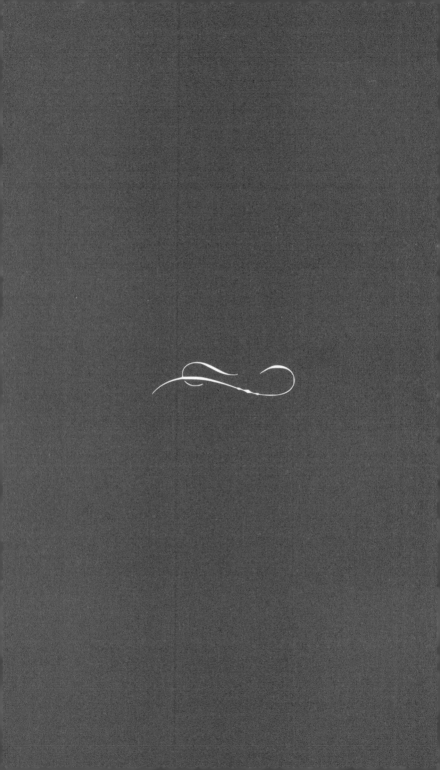

CHAPTER 2

It took longer than I expected to reach the house. The landscape was one of those deceptive ones, where you seem to be only a few hundred yards distant, but once you have picked your way through the hollows and wrinkles in the ground, you find that it's taken a quarter of an hour to get where you are going. Ground like that saved my life multiple times in the war, but I am still not fond of it. It always seems to be hiding things.

In this case, it was hiding no more than a hare, which stared at Hob and me with huge orange eyes as we rode past. Hob ignored it. Hares are beneath his dignity.

Reaching the house required crossing a short causeway over the lake, which Hob didn't enjoy any more than I did. I dismounted to lead him. The bridge looked sturdy enough, but the whole landscape was so generally decrepit that I found myself trying not to put my full weight down as I crossed, absurd as that sounds. Hob gave me the look he gives me when I am asking him to do something that he considers excessive, but he followed. The clop of his hooves sounded curiously flat, as if muffled by wool.

No one awaited me. The causeway led onto a shallow courtyard, set back from the rest of the building. On either side, the walls dropped directly into the lake, with only the occasional balcony to break up the lines. The front door was positively Gothic, probably literally as well as figuratively, a great monstrosity set into a pointed archway that would have been at home on any cathedral in Prague.

I took the great iron door knocker in hand and rapped on the door. The noise was so loud that I flinched back, half expecting the entire house to crumble at the vibration.

There was no answer for many minutes. I began to feel uneasy . . . surely Madeline could not have died in the time since her letter arrived? Was the household attending a funeral? (Which only goes to show you how the damned place acted on my nerves. I would not normally jump to *funeral* as my first guess.)

Eventually, long after I had given up hope and was eyeing the door knocker and wondering whether to make a second go of it, the door creaked open. An elderly servant peered around the door and stared at me. It was not an insolent stare so much as a puzzled one, as if I were not only unexpected but completely outside his experience.

"Hello?" I said.

"May I help you?" said the servant, at the same time.

We both paused, then I tried again. "I'm a friend of the Ushers."

The servant nodded gravely at this information. I waited, half expecting him to close the door again. But after a long, long moment, he finally said, "Would you like to come inside?"

"Yes," I said, aware that I was lying. I did not want to go into that tired house dripping with fungi and architectural eyes. But Madeline had summoned me and here I was. "Is someone available to tend to my horse?"

"If you will step inside, I will send the boy to attend to it." He opened the door, still not very wide. A shaft of gray daylight penetrated the darkness inside without illuminating much of anything. I walked down the shaft with my shadow taking point, and then the servant closed the door and I stood in darkness.

As leaden as the landscape outside had been, it was lit up like a burning city compared to the interior of the house. My eyes took a moment to adjust, and then there was a rasp of matches and the servant lit a set of candles on the side table by the door. He handed me one, as if it were completely normal for the house to be this dark at midday.

"Easton?" The voice was familiar, though the owner stood in the shadows of the hallway. "Easton, what are *you* doing here?"

I turned to face the owner of the voice just as he stepped forward. In the flickering light of the candle, I beheld my old friend Roderick Usher. He had been a friend of my youth and under my command in the war through an accident of fate. I knew his face as well as I knew my own.

And I swear to you, if I had not heard his voice, I would not have recognized him.

Roderick Usher's skin was the color of bone, white with a sallow undertone, a nasty color, like a man going into shock. His eyes had sunk into deep hollows tinged with blue and if there was a spare grain of flesh left on his cheeks, I couldn't see it.

The worst of it, though, was his hair. It floated in the air like spider silk, and I told myself that it was a trick of the candlelight that made it look white rather than blond. Either way, it was now all flyaway wisps, like strands of fog, drifting in a halo around his head. The very young and the very old have hair like that. It was unsettling to see it in a man a year my junior.

Both Roderick and Madeline had always been rather pale, even when we were children. Later, in the war, Roderick could be relied upon to burn rather than tan. They both had large, liquid eyes, the sort that are called doe-like by poets, although those poets have mostly never hunted deer, because neither of the Ushers had giant elliptical pupils and they both had perfectly serviceable whites. I could see rather too much of the whites of Roderick's eyes right now, in fact. His eyes gleamed feverishly in that unnaturally pale face.

"Usher," I said, "you look like you've been dragged arse-first through hell."

He gave a choked laugh and clutched at his head. "Easton," he said again, and when he lifted his head, there was a little more of the Roderick I knew in his expression. "Oh God, Easton. You have no idea."

"You'll have to tell me," I said. I put an arm around his shoulders and thumped him, and there was no flesh on his bones at all. He'd always been rawboned, but this was something else again. I could feel individual ribs. If Hob had ever looked like that, I'd challenge the stable master to pistols at dawn. "My God, Roderick, I don't think much of your cook if they let you go around looking like this."

He sagged against me for a moment, then straightened and stepped back. "Why did you come?"

"Maddy sent me a letter saying that she was ill. . . ." I trailed off. I did not want to say that Maddy had written that Roderick thought she was dying. It was too bald a statement and he looked like a shattered man.

"She did?" His eyes showed even more white around the edges. "What did she say?"

"Just that you were afraid for her health." When Roderick merely stared at me, I tried to make light of it. "Also her lifelong unrequited passion for me, of course. So naturally I came to sweep her off her feet and take her to live in my enormous castle in Gallacia."

"No," said Roderick, apparently ignoring my poor attempt at humor, "no, she cannot leave here."

"That was a joke, Roderick." I gestured with the candle. "I was worried, that was all. Do you want to keep standing in the hall? I've been on horseback all day."

"Oh . . . yes. Yes, of course." He passed a hand across his forehead. "I'm sorry, Easton. It's been so long since I've had visitors that I've forgotten all my manners. Mother would be ashamed." He turned, gesturing to me to follow him.

None of the halls were lit and all were cold. The lack of light did not seem to bother Roderick. I hastened to keep up, even with the candle. The floors looked black in the gloom, and I caught glimpses of ragged tapestries on the walls and carvings on the ceiling that belonged to the same Gothic sensibility as the door.

We turned into a newer wing of the building and I relaxed a little. Instead of tapestries, there were paneled walls, and some even had wallpaper. It was in poor condition, bubbled and swollen with damp, but at least it felt a little less like walking through an ancient crypt. Very few ancient crypts have plump shepherdesses and gamboling sheep on the walls. I consider this an oversight.

At last we reached a door that actually had light streaming under it. Roderick pushed open the door to a parlor with an actual fireplace, and though the windows were covered in moth-eaten curtains, a little light leaked around their edges as well.

There were several sofas drawn up close to the fire, and I got my second shock of the day, for reclining against one lay Madeline.

She was swathed in gowns and blankets, so I could not see if she was as emaciated as Roderick, but her face had become so thin that I could nearly see the bones under the skin. Her lips were tinged with violet, like a drowning woman's. I told myself it was some poorly chosen cosmetic, and then she stretched out a hand like a bird's claw to me, and I saw that her fingernails were the same deep cyanotic violet.

"Maddy," I said, taking her hand. Thank God for the time they spend hammering manners into officers, because it was only reflex that let me bow over her wrist and say, in a reasonably normal tone of voice, "It has been so very long."

"You haven't aged a day," she said. Her voice was weak, but still very much the Maddy I remembered.

"You have grown more beautiful," I said.

"And you have grown into an outrageous liar," she said, but she smiled as she said it, and a tiny bit of color came into her cheeks.

I released her hand and Roderick pointed me to the other person in the room, whom I had barely noticed in my alarm over Maddy. "May I present my friend James Denton?"

Denton was a tall, lanky man with silvering hair, probably

approaching fifty if not quite over the edge. He wore his clothes as if they were clothes rather than symbols of rank, and his mustache was too long for fashion.

"How do you do?" Denton said.

Ah. American. That explained the clothes and the way he stood with his legs wide and his elbows out, as if he had a great deal more space than was actually available. (I am never sure what to think of Americans. Their brashness can be charming, but just when I decide that I rather like them, I meet one that I wish would go back to America, and then perhaps keep going off the far edge, into the sea.)

"Denton, this is my sister's friend Lieutenant Easton, most recently of the Third Hussars."

"A pleasure, sir," I said.

I offered Denton my hand, because Americans will shake hands with the table if you don't stop them. He took it automatically, then stared at me, still holding my fingers, until I let them drop.

I knew the look, of course. Another classification, though not so graceful as Miss Potter's.

Americans, so far as I know, have no sworn, but I am given to understand that they have very lurid periodicals. Denton likely thought that a sworn soldier would be a seven-foot-tall Amazon with one breast cut off and a harem of cowed men under kan heel.

He was likely not expecting a short, stout person in a dusty greatcoat and a military haircut. I no longer bother to bind my breasts, but I never had a great deal to worry about in that direction, and my batman sees that my clothing is cut in proper military style.

Denton was not a swift social thinker, I gather, or perhaps he was thinking of the periodicals. I could see Roderick over his shoulder, tensing in case his guest should commit some serious faux pas. It took Denton a moment to clear his throat and say, "Lieutenant Easton, a pleasure. I beg your pardon, my country was not in the recent war, so I fear I have not had the privilege of serving alongside your countrymen."

"Fortunate America," I said dryly. "The Gallacian army . . . well, there are just about enough of us left to fill out a regiment, if you don't look too closely. I cashed out when it became obvious that they were more interested in filling overfed noblemen's private coffers than in rebuilding the ranks—and now *I* shall have to beg *your* pardon, Sir Roderick, Maddy, for speaking ill of your peers!"

Roderick laughed, with a little too much relief, and I took the glass of spirits that his servant was handing me. "I would forgive you gladly," he said, "if there was anything to forgive. What happened there was a great crime, and I'm grateful you will still have anything to do with those of us above the salt."

"How could I not?" I said, saluting Madeline with two fingers on the rim of my glass. "But what is the trouble of which you wrote?"

Maddy's flush had begun to fade, and this drove the last of it from her cheeks until she, too, was white as bone. "Perhaps we might speak of it later," she murmured, looking down at her hands.

"Yes, of course," I said. "Whenever you like."

Denton glanced from her to me and back again. I could see the wheels working in his head, trying to determine my relationship to his friend's sister. It was vaguely amusing and vaguely offensive all at once.

On the whole, I much preferred Eugenia Potter's swift classification. In some ways, it is rather refreshing to be treated in the same way as a fungus, though I might have felt differently if she insisted on taking spore prints or seeing what color I bruised.

"I am tired," said Madeline abruptly. Roderick leapt up and helped her to the door, and seeing them together, it struck me again just how badly they had both fared. Madeline had been a slender, pale-haired wisp of a girl, and she seemed to have aged forty years, though I knew it had been less than twenty. Roderick had aged better, except for his hair. It was his manner that had not fared so well. Madeline moved slowly, like an invalid, but Roderick was full of shuddering, nervous energy. He could not keep his fingers still, moving them restlessly on the arm of her dressing gown as if playing a musical instrument. He turned his head repeatedly to the side, as if listening for something, but there was no sound that I could hear.

I could not have said, as they both moved toward the door, which of them was leading the other.

They were but a moment gone when Denton said, quietly, "Shocking, isn't it?"

I looked at him sharply. "It's all right," he said, leaning forward. "Her rooms are a long way. We have a little time."

"I wish that they were closer, that she not have to walk so far," I said. "She is not well."

"Neither of them are," said Denton. "But there are only so many rooms in this great hulk that can be heated."

This I understood. My mind flashed back to my childhood home, to my mother wringing her hands over the price of coal, to rooms half-closed with sheets to save warmth.

"I have not seen Roderick in—oh, four or five years, I should think," said Denton. "I do not know how long it has been for you. . . ."

"Longer," I said, staring into my drink. Amber swirled in the firelight, and I fought down the urge to go and bank the fire to save wood. It would only hurt Roderick's pride.

It had been far too long since I had seen either of them. In Gallacia, they had lived nearby with their mother, who had always refused to live in the ancestral home. Having seen the place now, I was impressed she stayed here long enough to catch pregnant, or perhaps she did that during the honeymoon and took one look at the house and fled. Since Roderick had inherited, I had not seen them at all.

"So I will tell you, then, this is a recent dissolution," said Denton. "He has always been thin, but not like *this.*"

"His hair," I murmured. "I remember him being fair, like his sister, but . . ."

Denton shook his head. "Not like this," he said again. "I thought perhaps some nutritional malady, but I have seen the meals he eats, and they are sparse but not unhealthful."

"Something environmental, perhaps? This place . . ." I gestured vaguely with my free hand, but it was the tarn that I was thinking of, the dark water and the stinking fungus. "I think it might be enough to make anyone ill."

Denton nodded. "I've suggested he leave, but Miss Usher cannot travel. And he will not leave while she lives."

I sat up straighter in the chair. "Her letter said that Roderick thinks she is dying."

"Don't you?"

I drained the glass and Denton refilled it. "I've been here hardly above an hour. I hardly know what I think yet." And yet, the sight of Madeline had shocked me. *Dying.* Yes. It looked like death.

I did not know how to deal with this sort of death, the one that comes slow and inevitable and does not let go. I am a soldier, I deal in cannonballs and rifle shots. I understand how a wound can fester and kill a soldier, but there is still the initial wound, something that can be avoided with a little skill and a great deal of luck. Death that simply comes and settles is not a thing I had any experience with. I shook my head. "He'd mentioned something about the estate being in poor shape, but . . ." I lifted my hands helplessly. Probably there's a country where people aren't embarrassed to be poor, but I've yet to travel there. Of course Roderick would not have mentioned the shocking state of the house. "I assume the place is entailed and can't be sold?"

"He can't sell it, but I've begged him to leave it. Offered to let him stay with me, even. But he kept saying his sister could not travel."

I exhaled. That was probably true. Madeline looked as if a strong breeze might shatter her. I stared into my brandy, wondering what the hell to do.

"Forgive me if I was rude earlier," said Denton. "I've never met a sworn soldier before."

"That you know of," I said, sipping the brandy. "We don't all wear the pin."

That set him back for a moment. "I . . . no. I suppose not. May I ask—I'm sorry—why did you swear?"

There are two kinds of people, I have discovered, who will ask you these questions. The rarer, and by far the more tolerable, are seized with an intense curiosity about everyone and everything. "A sworn soldier! Really!" they will say. "What does that involve?" And five minutes later, someone will mention that their cousin is a vintner, and they will transfer all their attention to that person and begin interrogating them about the minutiae of winemaking.

I served with a man like this, Will Zellas, who was equally

fascinated by the stars, herbs, shoemaking, and battlefield surgery. I have always regretted that he was not with me to hear the remarkable maggots-and-piss speech from the shepherd. By then, alas, Will had taken a bullet to his shin, and had been in hospital. The last time I saw him, he walked with a cane and told me at extraordinary length about wood carving, the decline of the turnspit terrier as a breed, and how they harvest water lilies in India. His wife would inter- rupt occasionally to say, "Eat, dear," and he would manage about three bites before he was off again.

And then, of course, there are the other sort. They ask questions, but what they really want to know is what's in your pants and, by extension, who's in your bed.

I shall assume, gentle reader, that you are of the former sort and explain, in the event that you have not encountered Gallacia's sworn soldiers, or have only read of us in the more lurid periodicals.

As I mentioned before, Gallacia's language is . . . idiosyn- cratic. Most languages you encounter in Europe have words like *he* and *she* and *his* and *hers*. Ours has those, too, al- though we use *ta* and *tha* and *tan* and *than*. But we also have *va* and *var, ka* and *kan,* and a few others specifically for rocks and God.

Va and *van* are what children use before puberty, and also priests and nuns, although they're *var* instead of *van*. We have the equivalent of *boy* and *girl* and so forth, too, but using *ta* or *tha* to refer to a child is in incredibly poor taste. (If you are attempting to learn Gallacian and accidentally do this, immediately express that you are bad at the language and that you did not mean it, or else expect mothers to snatch their children up and look at you like a pervert.)

You can usually catch a Gallacian native speaker out by

the way that they will hesitate before using *he* or *she, él* or *ella,* or whatever the linguistic equivalent is, on a minor or a priest. At least one of our spies got caught that way during the war. And it's not unheard of for siblings to refer to each other as *va* for their entire lives.

And then there's *ka* and *kan.*

I mentioned that we were a fierce warrior people, right? Even though we were bad at it? But we were proud of our warriors. Someone had to be, I guess, and this recognition extends to the linguistic fact that when you're a warrior, you get to use *ka* and *kan* instead of *ta* and *tan.* You show up to basic training and they hand you a sword and a new set of pronouns. (It's extremely rude to address a soldier as *ta.* It won't get you labeled as a pervert, but it might get you punched in the mouth.)

None of this might have mattered, except for two or three wars before this one. We had entered into various alliances and suddenly they were getting invaded and we had to send our soldiers to defend them. And then one day it looked like we might get invaded ourselves, and we were running low on soldiers, and a woman named Marlia Saavendotter walked down to the army base and informed them that she was now a soldier.

All the official forms, you see, said nothing about whether you were male or female. They just said *ka.* Now, everybody knew that women were not allowed to be warriors, never had been, but this wasn't written down on the forms anywhere and an army runs on bureaucracy. They couldn't find a form to tell her that she couldn't sign up. A hundred years earlier, they would have just laughed *kan* out of the barracks, but they were incredibly shorthanded and here was a tough-looking person who could use a matchlock, and so the officer in charge decided that they would absolutely send Saavendotter home, but maybe not until after they had some more recruits to fill out the ranks. Except the other recruits never arrived and Saavendotter told kan friends and suddenly the Gallacian home army was about a third folks who had previously not been considered eligible but who were now kan through and through, and stayed that way until the war was over.

By that point, it would have been extremely difficult to tell everyone to go home, although people certainly tried. A bunch of arguments were had about it, and some very dramatic speeches were made on the steps of the capitol, including the famous "I am not a woman, I am a soldier!" speech that you've probably read about even if you know nothing else about Gallacian history. Inheritance laws were also involved in some fashion—I'm hazy on that bit—and after the dust settled, Gallacia had sworn soldiers. Now you walk in and take an oath that you're a soldier, they stamp a form, give you a pin so that people know to address you as *ka*, and then hand you a rifle and send you to the drill sergeant. And that's pretty much it. You get your head shaved, same as everybody. The uniform's the same as everyone else's. (There was a very brief attempt to make dress uniform an actual dress. It didn't end well.) The system still has a lot of blind spots and translating anything into another language gets complicated, but it works about as well as anything in the army, which is to say, despite everything.

People join for all reasons. There are people who really, really don't want to be women and this is the best option. There are people who want to get out of the mountains and this way you get a bed and a meat meal twice a week. And then there's me.

"Eh," I said, shrugging. "Someone had to send money home for my family. And my father, before he died, was a soldier, so it was in the blood, I suppose."

"But the war," said Denton. "Weren't you frightened?"

Sometimes it's hard to know if someone is insulting or just an American. Fortunately at that moment the door opened as Roderick returned, and I was able to turn it back. "Frightened? Hey, Roderick, were we frightened in Belgium?"

"Scared witless," said Roderick. He had been looking pensive when he entered the room, but the question seemed to cheer him. "Except when we were bored, which was most of the time."

"You served together, then?" said Denton.

I grinned. "Yes, and quite a shock it was to Roderick to show up and discover he'd been assigned to my unit. Though he hid it well enough."

"I figured I'd save all the sordid details of our youth for blackmail material. Though I wound up not needing it." He nodded to Denton. "I was only in for a year or two. Then Father died and I had to sell out. Easton stayed in a great deal longer."

"You were the smart one," I said. The war had been hard on my feet and my knees and my faith in humanity. But then my sister married a kind soul and was doing well, and I didn't need to send money home any longer, so I sold my commission. (Once you leave, incidentally, it's up to you what anyone calls you. Roderick went back to using *he*. After fifteen years in uniform, though, *ka* was just who I was.) "What did those extra years get me, except a bad shoulder and a good horse?"

"Shoulder still bothering you, then?"

"Eh." I shrugged, then winced dramatically, clutching my shoulder, and grinned at Roderick.

Denton's eyebrows drew together. "You were wounded?"

"Denton is a doctor," said Roderick. "It's part of why I asked him to come here."

Denton lifted a hand in protest. "Barely that," he said. "I had one year of schooling and then the South took it in its head to secede, and I was shoved out the door with a bonesaw and a sheet of paper saying I knew how to use it."

"Were you frightened?" I asked, with gentle malice.

His eyes flicked to me, acknowledging the hit, and his mustaches moved over a smile. I waited for him to demur, but he surprised me. "I was," he said. "All the time. We had to amputate so often, and I was always afraid they would die on the table. I knew most of them would die anyway, but if they died in front of me, it felt worse."

I winced. Our periodicals aren't nearly so lurid over here, but we'd still heard grim stories about doctors hacking off diseased limbs, dumping whiskey on the stump, and then having the next man brought in. If he'd even been on the outskirts of that, then Denton had been through hell a few times over.

"You sell yourself short," said Roderick. "I'd trust you over half the doctors in Paris."

"Ah, you only say that because I pour liquor over everything." He turned back to me. "Shoulder wound?"

"Musket ball, of all things," I said. "Someone had dug their grandfather's musket out of the attic and took a potshot at us as we came through. I was damned lucky, although I didn't feel that way at the time."

Denton winced. "Hit the bone?"

"Cracked it but didn't break it. The advantage to getting shot with an antique."

He nodded. "Fortunate. Insomuch as getting shot is ever fortunate."

Roderick started in with a story of a fellow we served with who was shot in the family jewels and went on to have three children. It's a good story. Denton winced in the appropriate places and we drank and sat by the fire and told war stories as if everything was completely normal and no one in the house was dying.

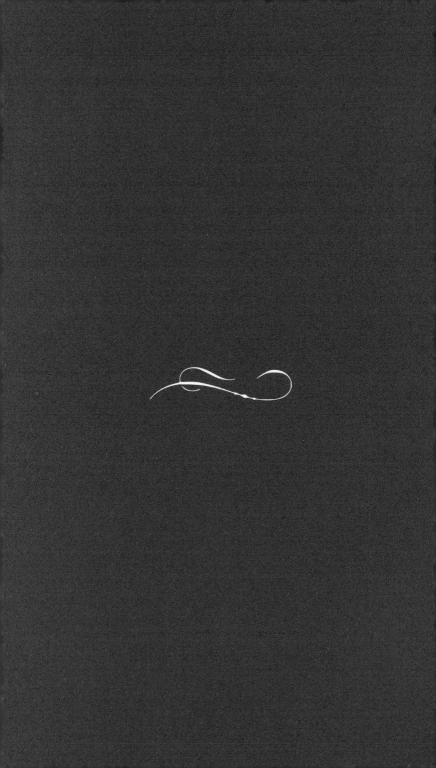

CHAPTER 3

When it was finally late enough that I was yawning, Roderick walked me to my rooms. This time he took a candle, and went more slowly.

"Did Denton insult you?" he asked, once we were out of earshot of the parlor. I could tell he was genuinely worried. "He's a good man, but you know they don't have sworn soldiers in America. I'll have a word with him if he did."

I shook my head. "Just the usual sort of thing. He'll settle down in a day or two, I imagine."

Roderick sighed. "I'm sorry. I know how tired you are of that."

I snorted. I'd been tired of it a decade ago. Now I'd moved to some other state entirely. Transcendent exhaustion, perhaps. Which had less to do with Dr. Denton and more to do with the ten thousand or so people before him. "I did not mean to surprise you and your guest, Roderick."

"No, no." The shadows jumped on the wall with the tremor of Roderick's hand. "I was ungracious before. I'm sorry. Of course you would come when you thought Madeline was . . . was ill. I should have realized."

"We were friends, once," I said quietly. "I hope we still are."

"Yes. *Yes.*" He turned to me almost eagerly, and I tried not to recoil at the way the candle cast deep shadows across his eye sockets and the gaunt planes of his face. "We were. We *are*. You led the charges. You knew what had to be done and you did it. I . . . I could use that now. I no longer know what needs to be done."

"We'll figure it out. It can't be worse than facing a line of rifles."

"Can't it?" Roderick blinked at me. "This place . . . this place . . ." He gestured with the candle. I followed the gesture to where wallpaper had peeled back from the walls, hanging in rags, leaving the exposed flesh of the building behind. Mold crept up the pale boards, tiny spots of black that joined together like constellations. "I hear things now," he said. "Everything. My own heartbeat. Other people's breathing sounds like thunder. Sometimes I fancy I can hear the worms in the rafters."

"It's a holdover from the war," I said, thinking of my own tinnitus. "Too many shells, too many bullets. We're all half-deaf and hearing things."

"Perhaps. But I hate this place," he said, almost dreamily. "And I am so afraid. I was never afraid like this during the war."

"We were younger then," I said. "And immortal."

He forced a smile. It was ghastly and I looked away, back to the moldering wallpaper. "Perhaps that's it. But this place has made me afraid. This dreadful house. I think I would rather face a line of rifles, even now. At least that's a human enemy."

I had no idea what to make of this talk. "We'll figure it out," I said again, firmly.

"I hope so. Everything frightens me now." He shook his head and laughed, and it was almost as ghastly as his smile. "I am not the soldier I was."

"None of us are what we were," I said, and let him show me to my room.

Breakfast was early. There were eggs and toast and black tea and little else on the sideboard. I took three eggs and felt immediately guilty for imposing so on Roderick's hospitality. Was there some way to make it up to him without appearing to offer charity? Bring in a deer, say, or a brace of partridge?

I sat with my tea, dipping my toast in the egg yolk, contemplating how one might increase the contents of the larder without it being obvious, when Denton came in. I nodded to him. He grunted. Not a morning person. That was fine, I wasn't either. I waited until he'd had his second cup of tea before asking the question I'd wanted to ask last night.

"Do you know what's wrong with Madeline?" I asked. "Medically?"

Denton raised his eyes blearily from his tea. "You don't pull punches in the morning, do you, Lieutenant?"

I began to apologize, but he waved it off.

"No, it's fine. I won't know any more when I'm awake than I do now. Hysterical epilepsy is probably the diagnosis she'd be given in Paris, for all the good it does."

"Hysteria?"

"Yes. Which is a useless damn diagnosis." He poured himself another cup of tea and offered me what was left of the teapot. I took it, even though the tea had steeped to bitterness. "Hysteria is like consumption used to be. Something wrong with you that we can't seem to fix? It's probably consumption. Now Koch has isolated the bacillus responsible for tuberculosis and we don't have that to lean on any longer, so we have to admit that there are people dying of something that isn't tuberculosis." He slugged back his tea and grimaced. "But we still have hysteria, although Monsieur Charcot tells us it's in men as much as women. Do we know the cause? No. Do we know how to treat it? No. Is it probably a dozen different disorders lumped under one name? Almost certainly. Don't ask me. I'm good with a bonesaw and I'll pour brandy down your throat and over your stump, but disorders of the nerves are beyond me."

"How odd," I said. "Madeline never struck me as the nervous sort. Neither of them did. Though Roderick . . ." I remembered his air last night, his talk of fear and the dreadful house.

Denton gave me a meaningful nod, and I guessed that Roderick had expressed the same sentiments to him. "I can't say that you're wrong there," said Denton. "Particularly not of late. But I can tell you that Madeline has catalepsy."

"Catalepsy!"

Denton nodded glumly. "Severely. She falls into immobile states for hours, and they are getting worse. The most recent was only a few days ago, and it lasted nearly a day and a half. Her reflexes were gone, she was ice-cold, and I could only barely see traces of her breath on a mirror."

I slumped back in my chair. That must have been after Madeline had written to me. No wonder Roderick thought she was dying. "I had no idea."

"No reason you should have." Denton rubbed his hand

over his mustache. "Of course, that's a diagnosis of the symptom, not the cause. As for the cause . . . I don't know. She's anemic and doesn't eat enough."

I looked over the spread of food. "Perhaps I'll go hunting, if Roderick does not object."

"I would have myself, but I'm a dismal shot."

I smiled. "Well, I am terrible at sewing people up after they've been shot, so I suppose it all works out." I pushed away from the table and went to go see what equipment I had to work with.

Predictably, I got lost. The house was a maze, and I hadn't seen it well the night before. I had only found the breakfast room by following the smell of toast. Eventually I saw a set of shuttered doors, half ajar, which seemed to indicate a balcony. Possibly if I got outside, I could figure out where in the building I was. Failing that, maybe I could climb down and walk to the front door.

When I reached the balcony, however, I found that it was already occupied.

In daylight, Madeline looked twice as shocking. Her hair was a dandelion's colorless wisp and her skin looked almost transparent. When she stood against the sun, I half expected to see light stream through her like a stained-glass window, with a frame of bones instead of lead.

"The lake is lovely, is it not?" she said, looking down over the water.

"Mountain lakes so often are," I said, which was true, even if this particular one was not. It looked dark and stagnant. *Lovely* is not the word I would have used to describe it. *In need of fire and holy water*, perhaps. Could you even burn a lake? I know there was a river in America that caught fire once, and had made the papers as an amusing footnote about how the Yanks could even make water burn, but I vaguely recalled there had been some kind of chemicals involved.

"Dear Easton," said Madeline. "Do you remember when we went down to the river together and tried to catch fish?"

"I remember that I caught one," I said, "and your execrable cousin . . . what was van name? Sebastian? . . . tried to steal it."

"And you pushed van into the river." She wrinkled up her nose and giggled. I tried not to show how much the sound of her giggle shocked me. It sounded thin and papery, like an insect rubbing its legs together, not at all like I remembered.

"It was so much easier back then," said Madeline longingly. "We were all van together. So young and healthy and hopeful. Now look at me." She gestured to her face and body. "It's no wonder that Roderick thinks I'm dying, when I look like this."

"How do you feel?" I asked, seizing upon the opening.

"Do you know, I feel quite energetic at times? I know that I look a fright. My mirror doesn't lie. No, he is quite right. I don't have much longer. But I did not think I would feel so restless."

I studied her face. She was still paler than any living being had a right to be, but there were two spots of color on her cheek, high and hectic. I was struck by a feeling that her skin was nearly transparent and if I were standing closer, I could have seen the individual tiny capillaries filled with blood. Her eyes were feverishly bright, but when I had touched her hand earlier, it had been as cold as the waters of the tarn.

Catalepsy. Anemia. "You should leave here," I said abruptly.

"This place can't be healthy. Let Roderick bring you back to Paris. We'll go to the theater and the museums and walk in the parks and eat lemon ice."

She smiled, though it seemed like she was not looking so much at me as through me, and smiling at whatever she saw on the far side. "Lemon ice. I remember. We had them the last time I saw you, before you swore as kan."

I had no real memory of what we'd eaten that day, but I agreed anyway. "We'll have it again."

"Ah, Easton." She patted my arm. Her hand felt chill, even through the sleeve. "You're kind. But I belong here. I would be lost if I could not go down to the lake and confess my sins."

"What sins could you possibly have?" I asked, trying to sound playful, not entirely succeeding. "You have always been above reproach. You did not even help me push your cousin into the river."

"Have I?" She looked through me again. "Perhaps it is only in dreams that I am sinning." She smiled again, but it turned into a yawn. "Forgive me, dear Easton. I am tired. I should go lie down for a little while."

"Let me walk you to your door," I said, offering her my arm. "You will have to tell me where it is, in this great maze of a house, but I will take you there."

She leaned on me. She weighed nothing at all. I saw her to her room, and she seemed to float through the door as if the earth could no longer quite hold her.

When I finally returned to my rooms, after trying three doors that looked right and weren't, I found a very welcome arrival. My batman, Angus, was already there.

"Angus!" I clasped his forearm. "You made it!"

"Aye," he said, fixing me with a gimlet eye. "A short journey with fresh horses over empty roads in decent repair. Truly it taxed me to my limits. Sir."

I grinned, unrepentant. Angus served my father before me, and even then was long in cunning, if not yet long in years. When my father was killed in battle and I swore in, he took one look at me, a callow fourteen-year-old with bound breasts and a freshly shaven skull, and took me in hand. "For," he said, "the Good Lord may look out for fools, but it won't hurt to have another set of eyes helping."

When I sold out my commission, he came with me. His beard and mustaches had gone entirely gray and he could predict the weather with pinpoint accuracy based on various aches and pains, but I would have put him up against any younger soldier I know, myself included.

He had a thick Scottish brogue when he chose to indulge in it, but could shed it instantly for unaccented Gallacian, and even I didn't know where it was he came from originally. He never expressed any desire to return. I had offered once, and it so offended him that I did not offer again.

"Should I be insulted by the room they've put you in, or are they doing the best they can?" he asked.

I glanced around the room. It wasn't much better by daylight than it had been by candlelight. The wallpaper was still mostly intact and the fireplace worked, but there was a creeping damp to the air. The great curtained bed sagged and the curtains were tattered to gauze. The door to Angus's room was swollen and stuck in the jamb. "I think it's the best they can do," I said. "And go easy on the fire, will you? I don't think they can afford the logs."

"So that's the way of it, eh?" Angus nodded. He helped

me out of my jacket and scowled at the room in general. "Cheerless house," he said. "I mislike it."

"You and me both," I said tiredly. "You know I'm not a superstitious soul, Angus, but I swear there's something wicked here."

"Well, I *am* a superstitious soul," said Angus, "and I *know* there is. It ain't canny. The sort of place you find devils dancing on the moors."

"There aren't any moors. There's a sort of heath and a tarn and a mad Englishwoman painting mushrooms."

He raised an eyebrow. I described the redoubtable Eugenia Potter.

"Oh, that sort!" he said, poking up the fire and turning the bricks to heat them. "One of the fine, fierce old ladies of England. They'll climb mountains and make tea on the summit if they need to. We'd have done a damn sight better in the war if they'd sent them over instead of the troops."

"Probably not a devil of the moors, then?"

"Well, I haven't met her yet. She might be." Angus sniffed. "Mushrooms, eh?"

"Yes, and some nasty ones, too. Poked one with a stick for me, and it smelled like an open grave and rotten milk. And she said it wasn't even ripe yet!"

"They say mushrooms spring up where the Devil walks," said Angus sourly. "*And* where fairies dance."

"Do you think they ever get the two confused? The Devil shows up to a fairy ball, or finds himself mobbed with elven ingénues?"

He gave me a look from under his eyebrows. "You shouldn't joke about fairies. Sir."

"Oh, very well. As long as I can still joke about the Devil."

He grunted, which was Angus-speak for not approving

but not caring enough to stop me. "The villagers don't like the place," he said.

I had passed through the village, but hadn't thought much about it. It didn't look bad. It didn't look good. It was a village. It looked like every other small village in Ruravia, which also look pretty much like every small village in Gallacia, although they carve flowers on their shutters here and we carve turnips. (That is a general *we*. I have never carved a turnip in my life.)

"Don't like the house? Or don't like the Ushers?"

"The house. If anything, I'd say they pity the current crop. Sir Roderick's great-uncle, or whoever he inherited this heap from, sold the people their land back before the creditors came for it, so they remember him fondly. '*Our* Usher,' they call him. And Sir Roderick's 'Young Usher.'"

"And Madeline?"

He gave me an opaque look. "'That poor Usher girl.'"

I sighed. Angus raised an eyebrow. "She's not looking well," I said, in response to the unspoken invitation. "I see why Roderick thought she was dying. I think she might be."

Angus is a sympathetic soul, particularly for women. "Ah, the poor lass," he said, and meant it. "This is no place for a delicate lady. I tell you, it's haunted, moor or not."

"Did the villagers tell you that?"

"You laugh, but aye, they did. I asked about hunting hereabouts, and they told me not to do it. Said the place is full of witch-hares."

"Witch-hares?"

"Aye. Familiars to devils. You shoot one and the next day you find a witch with a bullet in her heart."

"Hard luck for her. Are many little old ladies with warts

turning up with bullets in them around here? That really sounds like a job for the constabulary."

"Bah. Disbelieve me all you like. They say the hares don't act right, though. They forget how to run. The man at the inn, he said he'd walked right up to one once and it sat there and stared at him as if it had never seen a human man before."

"I assume a witch would have seen a man before, so I don't know if that goes to support your theory."

Angus drew himself up to his full height, which wasn't much, and full dignity, which was considerable. "'Tis not my place to speak on the habits of witches. But I'll not hunt hares here, I can tell you that much. Nor deer."

I raised an eyebrow. Angus is particularly fond of eating all of God's creatures, and this seemed like a great sacrifice. "How will you occupy your time, then?"

"I," said Angus, still with unassailable dignity, "plan to go fishing."

CHAPTER 4

So here I was. Roderick hadn't expected me, whatever that meant—possibly that he hadn't thought I was enough of a friend to come when he needed me, or perhaps he didn't think he needed me. Maybe he didn't. Denton didn't know what to make of me. Madeline was . . . yes, dying. I had looked in the faces of enough dying soldiers to know. Sometimes people surprise you, sometimes they pull through, but there is a particular waxiness to human skin that tells you when someone is not long for this world. Madeline's was starting to acquire that texture. If I came down to breakfast tomorrow and discovered that she had died during the night, I would not have been shocked. Saddened, but never shocked.

When I am perturbed, I like to walk. I feel slow and stupid when I sit, but walking seems to wake something up in my brain. I never minded pacing back and forth with a rifle on guard duty, because I could think more easily. Daydream, even, if I'm being honest. Mostly I daydreamed about the end of the war, about scenarios where all my people made it out alive and unharmed. It was only when we were pinned down and I could not walk that it became harder for me to keep those dreams alive.

I did not particularly wish to walk the halls of Usher's mansion. The tattered wallpaper, the specks of mold . . . Madeline with her feverish eyes and wisps of white hair . . . none of these were things I wished to encounter. So I rose early and saddled Hob and went out for a ride.

Hob greeted me more eagerly than usual, possibly because Denton's horse in the next stall was a terrible conversationalist, or perhaps because the stable was so gloomy. It was clean and fairly dry, but it had the same sullen air as the rest of the manor house.

The air of the heath was cool and damp. I might have found it oppressively silent under normal circumstances, but compared to what we had left behind, it felt free and open. Mist clung to the surface of the dark lake and gathered in hollows on the ground, but Hob cantered through them and broke them up like the shreds of bad dreams.

My thoughts, unfortunately, did not break up as easily. The Ushers were not well, any fool could see that. The house was obviously terrible for anyone who was sick. Miasma, as my great-grandmother would have said. Of course, it was 1890, and no one really believed in that anymore. It was all germs now, thanks to Dr. Koch. Still, germs could linger in a place, could they not? Was there enough disinfectant in the world to cleanse the house of Usher?

So. What did I do about it?

I couldn't very well kidnap the Ushers and drag them back to Paris at gunpoint. Madeline wouldn't survive. Roderick probably would, and be better for it, but Denton would undoubtedly object. And you can't exactly threaten to shoot someone to save their life. Angus would be extremely sarcastic if I tried.

Burning down the house of Usher, while tempting, had similar practical problems. I grimaced. Hob slowed down, feeling me shifting in the saddle, and put one ear back in inquiry.

"Sorry, boy," I said. "I'm not good company today."

Hob's ears were the equine equivalent of a shrug. Horses don't understand a lot about the world, but I have found that they sometimes understand particular humans terrifyingly well. Mules understand a lot more about the world, but less about humans—or possibly they just don't care what humans think. I'd buy either explanation, really.

We trotted across the countryside, steering clear of patches of the stinking redgills. They thinned out as we left the tarn behind, then began to increase again as I turned Hob back toward the manor house.

Where one finds mushrooms, one sometimes also finds redoubtable English ladies. I saw the umbrella first, then Miss Potter sitting under it. She had a sketchbook in her lap, and was staring intently at a brown lump.

I slid from Hob's back and looped his reins over the saddle. "Stand," I said. Hob gave me a look saying that this was unnecessary as there was nowhere in this desolate countryside he particularly wished to go.

Miss Potter dabbed carefully at the sketchbook. She was working from a small tin of pigments and I could see the pages of the book were wavy with the marks of watercolor washes.

"Unless it is urgent, officer, I will be with you in a few moments," she called. "The paint is wet and I do not wish it to dry before I have finished this study."

"Please, take your time," I said. "There is nothing so urgent that I would interrupt your painting."

She gave a short, occupied nod and bent over her watercolors.

Temporarily dismissed, I ambled over to the lake. The water was still dark and not entirely reflective. Patches seemed matte, as if the lake itself was moldering. The house squatted on the far side.

I picked up a pebble and tossed it into one of the matte places. It landed and sank, the ripples stopping almost instantly.

I tried skipping a rock across it. The first skip went well enough and left the correct ripples, but the second seemed to land in something gelatinous and the rock vanished into the water.

"Algae mats, I believe," said Miss Potter, coming up beside me. "The lake is full of them. How are you doing, Officer Easton?"

"Lieutenant Easton, please," I said. "Or simply Easton, if you like."

"Lieutenant." She inclined her head. I smiled. Most Englishwomen of my acquaintance would have to be pinned down by enemy fire for three days before they would consent to call a companion merely "Easton," and even then, they would revert to titles the moment anyone else was present.

The lake spread out at our feet. It was so still. I am used to tiny ripples in any body of water this size, and the flatness was unsettling. There was even a slight breeze that should have caused ripples, by rights. It tugged at my hair and set the ribbons on Miss Potter's hat dancing.

"Are there mushrooms underwater?" I asked abruptly.

I regretted it as soon as the words were out of my mouth. It seemed like a child's question. But Miss Potter did not treat it that way.

"A complex question. The simple answer is that we probably do not know of any."

"Probably?" I tilted my gaze toward her. She had a slight frown.

"Probably. The mycelium networks of mushrooms do not seem to enjoy being completely submerged. Several people have grown mushrooms on logs that were submerged in aquaria, but we must presume that the fungus itself was present in the log before it was placed in the water. Also . . ." Her frown shifted into what, in another woman, might have been a curled lip of disgust.

"Also?"

"There is an *American*," she said, pronouncing the word with distaste, "who claims to have seen gilled mushrooms in a river in their far west. But his report is unsubstantiated by any *reputable* observer."

It must have been terribly galling to be barred from an organization merely because one lacked the proper genitals, when disreputable Americans were allowed to join and write about underwater mushrooms. I had encountered Englishwomen with similar feelings about the military. One of them had gone on to move to Gallacia and swear as a soldier, and more power to kan.

"Is there some reason mushrooms wouldn't grow underwater? Besides the mycelium?"

"Spores float," said Miss Potter simply. "They might well

come to rest along the banks, but they could not sink to the bottom of the river to grow there. It would be like growing a coconut tree on the bottom of the ocean."

"Ah."

She tapped her parasol against the pebbles of the beach. "That said, mushrooms are not the only fungus. There are many, many types in the world. We walk constantly in a cloud of their spores, breathing them in. They inhabit the air, the water, the earth, even our very bodies."

I felt suddenly queasy. She must have read my expression, because a rare smile spread across her face. "Don't be squeamish, Lieutenant. Beer and wine require yeast, as does bread."

"Fair enough. So there is fungus in water, then?"

"Oh yes. A great deal of it. Mostly we recognize it when it becomes parasitic upon something else. Fish, for example. There are many fungi that plague the keepers of aquaria, causing growths upon their fish. It is not my field, but I know of three or four. Mostly they cause scabrous patches, but I have seen fungus that grows like a puff of cotton on the fins of fish, or sprouting forth from their mouth or lungs."

"How distressing," I said.

"Certainly for the fish, I would imagine. Though I do not know if fish have the intelligence to be distressed. Perhaps they simply believe that the fungus is part of them, and their fins have become larger."

I shook my head. "And is there fungus here, in the tarn?"

"Undoubtedly. You would likely require a microscope to observe it, however."

"I don't suppose you have one lying around, Miss Potter? In among your paints, perhaps?"

She smiled again, though fleetingly. "I fear they are beyond my means. I must content myself with a magnifying glass." She tapped her parasol again, in much the manner one might a cane. "You must think me a bit mad to be so obsessed with the kingdom of fungi, but it is a fascinating world. And an important one. Our civilization is built on the back of yeasts."

"I do not think you are mad at all," I said, which was true. "I enjoy the passions of others vicariously. One of the most pleasant interludes I have ever spent was listening to the treatise an aging shepherd once delivered to me on the inferiority of other breeds of sheep, and this has a much more general appeal."

"High praise." She hid a chuckle behind one gloved hand. I wished I dared to imitate the "piss 'n shit in th' flaps o' they hides!" speech for her, but I had no wish to alienate the redoubtable Miss Potter. I looked across the lake instead, and saw a pale white shape emerge from a little door near the lake. Madeline? It must have been, unless one of the servants wore white.

The shape made its way slowly down to the water, not stopping until it was at the edge. I could not make out whether or not it was actually touching the lake. I felt an urge to leap on Hob and ride back at a gallop to stop her from touching the water. Surely wet feet could do no good in her condition.

Surely that water could do no one any good, regardless of their condition. But what could I do?

Anemia, Denton had said. The treatment for anemia, so far as I knew, was good red meat. There was precious little of that in the house of Usher.

I didn't know how to fix catalepsy, but red meat I could manage. The only trick was how to get it into the larder.

I took my leave of Miss Potter, pausing to compliment her painting. She turned the compliment aside with a practiced air. "I'm well enough. You should see my niece Beatrix. Twice the talent, and an artist's eye. And a very gratifying interest in mycology."

I mounted my horse and rode back to the house, looking for Angus to put my plan into action.

"So we'll say you shot it," I said, as we approached the house that evening.

"Like hell we will," said Angus. "I'd take a bullet for you, same I did your father, but damned if I'll have you besmirching my shooting to a nob."

"He's not a nob, he's Roderick. We all had the runs together over the same trench."

"He's Lord Usher now, and I don't care how much shit we passed, I'll not take the blame for this one."

I drew breath to argue, but he added, "*And* I did the negotiatin', did I not?"

I sighed. His accent was getting thicker and that was never a good sign. "Fine, fine. Come in with me and make it convincing."

It had been a ridiculous plan, but straightforward enough. I walked into the parlor and found Roderick sitting alone at the piano, toying with the keys in a desultory fashion.

"Roderick," I said, "I fear I've got a confession to make."

He looked up, his pale eyebrows drawing together. "A confession? What do you mean?"

"Well. You know Angus and I went hunting this afternoon."

He nodded. "After birds, yes."

"Well . . ." I drew out the moment, took a deep breath, and said, "Roderick, I've shot a bloody cow."

Roderick stared at me blankly.

"I told kan it weren't never a deer," said Angus, his accent even more pronounced than usual. "But does ka listen to me? Me, who taught kan to shoot at me very knee?"

"It was one of the little brown ones they have around here!" I said, exasperated. (I didn't have to fake the exasperation. Angus was laying it on thick.) "They're deer-colored and it wasn't very big and it had its head down . . ."

"Those hip bones were never a deer! And did I not teach ye never to shoot afore ye had the shot absolutely clean? If you were a recruit, I'd box your ears for it. Better that than ye kill a man!"

"Regardless, I did *not* kill a man," I said frostily. I turned back to Roderick. "I paid the cow's owner twice what it was worth, but I'm terribly sorry if this makes trouble for you with your people. I genuinely thought it was a deer."

Angus muttered something into his mustache. Roderick's lips had begun to twitch and his shoulders shook.

"*Anyway,*" I said, giving Angus a hard look, "there'll be a delivery from the butcher in a day or so."

"From the butcher?" said Roderick, in a high, strangled voice.

I hunched my shoulders. Angus aimed a cuff at the back of my head. "Well an' I taught kan, ye eat what ye shoot! Yer no nob to go huntin' the little beasties for sport—begging pardon, Lord Usher—and leavin' t'poor creature where it falls!"

"He made me *field dress* the *cow*," I said to Roderick.

This was too much for my old friend. He let out a howl of

laughter and fell back against the piano, clutching his chest and gasping. I folded my arms and failed to smother a smile.

"Angus . . ." said Roderick, when he finally stopped laughing. "Angus, you old devil, you haven't changed by a hair. Field dressed the cow!" This set him off again.

"I," I said, with as much dignity as I could muster, "am going to go wash the cow off my boots. And trousers. And the rest of me." I stalked to the door, leaving Roderick collapsed over the piano. Angus followed me, uttering dark commentary on my field dressing of the cow, which, I wish to state for the record, was perfectly adequate.

"Phew," I said, when we were safely out of earshot. "That went well."

"Aye, the laugh'll do him good. And a good piece of beef'll do her ladyship good as well." Angus's accent had returned to its normal proportions. "Not a bad plan, youngster."

"It was a bloody stupid plan," I said, "but it did the job. I couldn't very well just have a side of beef delivered to the house."

"Pity you couldn't have got a younger one," said Angus, a bit sadly. "That cow they sold us will be tough as a boot."

"We will chew that boot with a glad heart."

"Oh aye, we will."

I endured a great deal of ribbing at dinner from Roderick and Denton, which I tolerated because it made Madeline laugh. "Now this," said Roderick, indicating the chicken on the table, "this is not a deer, Easton. I feel we must be clear on that."

"Perfectly."

"Nor am I a deer."

"No, of course not." I rolled my eyes at Madeline. "Deer are the ones that go moo."

She giggled. It was still the papery giggle of an invalid, but it was genuine humor and I'd take it.

She retired early, before it was barely dark. I hoped that once the butcher actually delivered the sacrificial cow, she'd be able to eat enough meat to do her good. I also sought my bed early, pleading exhaustion from the cow incident.

Two hours later saw me still awake, though. I kept mulling over something that the cow's owner had said to me earlier. I should have been able to dismiss it, but it stuck like an eyelash in the corner of my eye, minor but maddening.

We had finished the butchery—for all my complaints about field dressing, I'd had help, since cows are a great deal larger than deer—and the farmer's younger sons were carting loads of meat to the butcher. The farmer and his oldest son, nearly identical to his father, stood beside me, watching.

"Young man," said the cow's previous owner, and stopped.

I didn't bother to correct him. It's less galling to be mistaken for a man than a woman, for some reason. Probably because no one tries to kiss your hand or bar you from the Royal Mycology Society. And I am familiar with this sort of fellow, who are the salt of the earth and move on a similar geological time frame. I waited.

"You're not afraid of working," said the farmer at last, nodding to the wreckage of the cow.

I smiled. "I may be staying up at the manor house, but I'm no noble. I don't get to lie around eating peeled grapes."

"Mmm." He fixed me with a penetrating look. "Your man speaks well of you. Angus."

This was gratifying, but I didn't think the farmer had drawn me aside merely to pass on Angus's praise. I waited some more.

"Said you talked about hunting hares."

"I thought of it," I admitted. "A cow wasn't my first thought, and I'm grateful that you were willing to sell us one." I had also been grateful that Angus had located this man, who, he said, was not prone to gossip and would make sure that word of my clandestine arrangement to buy beef for the Usher larder would not get back to Roderick's ears.

He waved off my gratitude and lapsed back into silence. I gazed over the field, which was far healthier looking than the land around the manor house. I could hear insects singing in the grass, and a bird flitted among some low bushes at the edges.

"The hares around the lake aren't canny."

I tilted my head. "Angus said that he'd heard that. That they don't act right." I decided not to mention witch-hares, out of fear he'd think I was mocking him.

His son finally spoke up. "They're not so bad around here," he said. "But you go up toward the house and they get strange."

"Strange?" I asked. "Strange how?"

"They don't run," said the son. "If they move, it's slow. I walked right up to one once, and when it finally moved, it was like it didn't know how its legs worked. Fell over a few times."

"Sounds like a disease," I offered. *Please, God, let there not be a rabies outbreak up here, on top of everything else.*

"Not rabies. Rabies doesn't make them watch you." The farmer leveled a finger at me. "And they watch, all the time. Not the way hares stare at you and bolt if you move. They'll come up to you and watch. The missus saw one down here once, came right up to the dairy and stood and stared at her. She knew it was one of the ones from up by the lake by how it moved."

I rocked back on my heels, startled by this sudden flurry of words.

"I followed one once," said the son. "It'd get to walking pretty good and then it would miss a step and fall over and kick. It'd see a jump and it'd have to stop and think about how to go over it. Sometimes it didn't jump, just walked through the ditch. I just kept on to see where it was going."

"And where *was* it going?" I asked.

"Don't know," said the son. "Got to the lake and fell in. Couldn't seem to figure out how to swim. Just laid down on the bottom and drowned in three inches of water."

These were strange thoughts, but there was little that I could do about them. If some strange disease was afflicting the local hares, that was a job for a veterinarian rather than a veteran.

I was half asleep and headed for three-quarters when I heard a board creak in the hallway. It might not have registered except that a second board creaked a moment later, close enough that whoever was setting the boards creaking was moving very slowly indeed.

Someone was creeping down the hall. I catapulted into consciousness and reached for my sidearm on the nightstand.

There are people who sleep with a loaded gun under their pillow and I've nothing much to say about that, except that I would not choose to share a bed with them. When I was nineteen and had seen a few battles and thought myself very hardened and worldly, I myself slept with my sidearm under my pillow. This lasted until the night that the damn thing discharged under my ear. If I'd been sleeping with my head on the other half of the pillow, I would probably not be telling you this story now, but I escaped unharmed. The pillow exploded into a blizzard of feathers and the bullet took out the lamp and buried itself in the closet door. I had just enough presence of mind to grab my luggage before I was thrown out into the street by the proprietress, who screamed at me for five minutes straight. Unfortunately for her, I was completely deafened and so missed the nuance of her diatribe, but the hand gestures were very clear. My tinnitus probably dates to this particular episode, and thus I cannot blame anyone for it but myself.

I opened the door a crack and peered both ways. No one . . . except for an instant, I thought I saw a white form trailing out of sight around a corner.

I have, as I have told you, reader, the psychic sensitivities of mud. It did not occur to me that I might be hallucinating, or that I might be seeing a ghost. Someone was walking through the halls at night and that someone must be real and alive.

And yet, having said this, I must admit that something must have been acting on my nerves, because why else would I have gone in pursuit, holding a loaded pistol? It was more than likely a servant. Servants are up at all hours, making sure that everyone's shoes are blackened and the fires are laid. Granted, I had so far only seen one servant, but presumably there were more. So why did I automatically assume it was an intruder?

I moved as stealthily as I could, which was not very. The

black boards creaked and yawned underfoot. I might as well have hired a brass band to play a march. When I rounded the corner, there was no one there.

Doorways lined the hall, and there was a stairway down to the lower floor. The person might have gone anywhere. I strained my ears for the creak of floorboards, and instead got a wave of tinnitus ringing over me. (My own damn fault. Listen too hard, tense the wrong muscles in my jaw, and it kicks off every time. Which you'd think I'd know by now.)

The ringing faded. I stood in the dark with my pistol braced against nothing, and then crept back to bed, feeling foolish indeed.

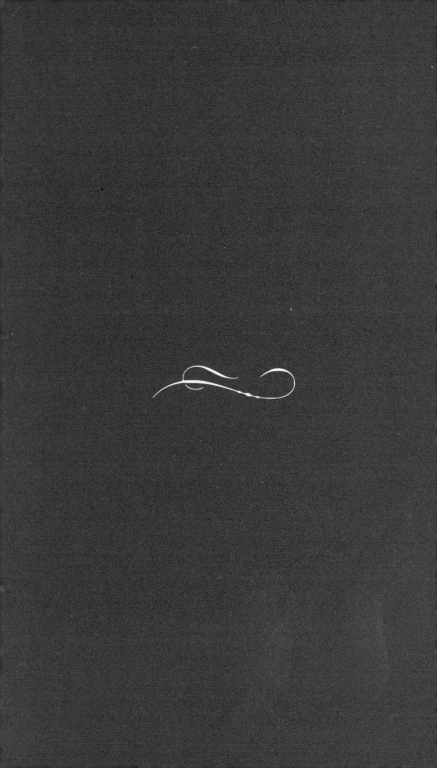

CHAPTER 5

I slept late the next day. Butchering a cow is no joke. I rode out on Hob, and Denton joined me on his gelding, which resembled a piece of overstuffed furniture with ears. I had the pleasure of introducing Denton to the redoubtable Miss Potter, who was taking a spore print of a mushroom.

"Ah," she said, leaning on her furled umbrella. "A doctor, are you?"

"Of medicine, not mycology, I fear," I said. Denton had the grace to look abashed. Miss Potter generously forgave him both this failing and his poor luck to hail from America, with its spurious claims of underwater mushrooms.

"Here attending Usher's sister?" she asked.

If Denton was surprised at the speed at which gossip carries across the heath, he did not show it. "For all the good I do," he said. "It is God's hands, not mine. Perhaps not even His."

If this impiety shocked her, Miss Potter gave no sign. She nodded gravely and changed the subject. Admittedly, she changed it to fungi, but I was willing to accept it. Denton also requested a demonstration of the stinking redgill, and this time, I stayed very well back and held the horses.

No pantomime players could have improved upon the play—Miss Potter, resolute, Denton staggering backward and throwing his sleeve across his face as if struck by acid. I enjoyed it enormously.

It was as I was leading the horses toward them, after the smell had time to dissipate, that I saw another hare sitting up in the grass.

I looked at it. It looked at me. It seemed completely normal as hares go, which is to say half-starved, with staring orange eyes. If it had some strange malady, it was not immediately visible.

"Are you a witch, then?" I asked the animal, half-amused.

I was not expecting an answer and I didn't get one. It sat up on its hind legs with its forepaws against its chest and simply watched.

"Go on, shoo," I said, waving a hand toward it. "Before I forget that I told Angus I wouldn't hunt hares."

It didn't move.

I stamped a foot at it. It still didn't move.

March hares are all mad, of course, but it wasn't March and their madness tends to be much more active—leaping and boxing and bounding in all directions. This one was so still that if the breeze had not moved its fur, I would think it might be dead. It did not even twitch its ears. I had not seen it blink.

I took a few steps toward it, and finally it did move, but not like any four-legged animal I'd ever seen. It put out one front foot and seemed to drag itself forward, then the other. Then one hind foot, catching up, then the other. It looked like a man scaling a sheer cliff, but on level ground. Then it turned and sat up again, watching me.

"Have you no sense, hare?" I asked.

Its unblinking orange eyes held no answer.

Before I could do something thoroughly rash, like shoot it—and the thought was starting to cross my mind—Miss Potter and Denton reappeared. "Talking to yourself, Easton?" asked Denton.

"Talking to a hare," I said, pointing, but when I looked back, the animal was gone.

The butcher was as good as his word and the first of the beef graced the table that night. As Angus had predicted, it was tough as boot leather, but the cook managed to make a broth and I saw with pleasure that Madeline took more of it than she had of the chicken that we had eaten for the past few nights.

Angus growled something when I came in. He looked surly, even by Angus standards.

"No luck fishing today?"

"Oh, I had luck, aye, if you can call it that," he said. His mustaches bristled like an angry hedgehog. "Caught a fine fish. Only it weren't so fine after all."

"You've lost me, Angus."

"Had a gob of stuff trailing out of it," he said. "Thought t'were fish shit, and then thought maybe t'were its guts coming out."

"Good God, man, what are you using for fishhooks if you're gutting the fish with them?"

"My hook," he said, with dignity, "were in the fish's mouth where t'were supposed to be. As clean a cast as ever made, and reeled in proper. I gutted it and it were all through with stuff like slimy felt, including a string hanging out its arse."

This sounded quite disgusting, and I told Angus as much.

"Yes," he said. "Something wrong with the damn fish is what it is. I caught up a second one and what do you think I saw?"

"Slimy felt?"

"Gobs." He folded his arms.

"Fish are slimy little devils to begin with," I started to say, but Angus shot me a withering look with both eyes and mustache and I relented. Angus would know the difference between regular slime and something unusual. I remembered Miss Potter talking about fungus that attacked the fish in aquaria. "Could be a fungus. I can ask Miss Potter about it, if you like. Or you can ask her yourself. So far as I know, she's the only Englishwoman stomping about the place looking at mushrooms."

"We exchanged a wave," said Angus. "I didn't go bothering her, and she didn't go bothering me."

"A wave, though! From an Englishwoman, that's practically a hearty handshake. She only deigned to speak to me because I was about to poke a mushroom with a stick."

"The Good Lord looks out for fools. In your case, apparently He sends the occasional Englishwoman."

"I thought He'd sent you."

"You're a two-person job, youngster."

A thought struck me. "You didn't eat the fish, did you?"

"Great blistering Christ, of course not. D'ye take me for an idjit?"

I am occasionally deficient in tact, but I knew better than

to answer that. "Never," I said, and retired to my bedchamber, while Angus muttered and grumbled about witch-hares and fish on strings. (I thought of telling him about my encounter with the hare, but what could I say? It looked at me funny? The way it moved was rather horrible?)

It was cold in the room and I was still half-dressed when I heard another soft creak of boards as someone passed my door. This time I leapt out of bed, ignoring stealth entirely, and flung the door open.

There! A white shape, just vanishing. I snatched up a candle and bolted after it, reaching the corner where I had lost it the night before, and saw it, ghost-pale in the dark. It did not enter any of the doors, but moved purposefully toward the stairwell.

A figure clad in white, I thought. Not a servant, unless Roderick had given his servants a uniform more akin to a burial shroud. It carried no candle, but shuffled along, steps oddly halting and yet moving swiftly for all of that, unbothered by the dark.

It paid no attention to me as I approached. It was descending the stairs when I finally caught up to it and could make out features beyond ghostly whiteness. White hair, flowing white cloth, skin so pale it was almost transparent . . .

"Madeline?" I asked.

She wore a night rail with small, high sleeves. Until that moment, I had not realized quite how much weight she had lost. The garment hung off her, and what might have been modest enough on a larger woman now fell well below her collarbone. The openings for her arms seemed to gape open, revealing a glimpse of her ribs. I prayed that it was the shadows that made them seem to stand out so far from her skin.

She took another shuffling step downward, her hands

hanging limply at her sides. Her eyes were open, sweeping from side to side, though I could not tell if they were focused. Was she sleepwalking?

"Madeline . . ." I glanced around, hoping that no one else would come along and see her in this state of undress. Certainly not Denton or even Angus. "Madeline, can you hear me?"

She did not reply. Conventional wisdom was that you never wake a sleepwalker, but conventional wisdom had not allowed for a woman walking in the dark in a house with bad floors and a ruined wing and balconies that led directly to a thirty-foot drop into a lake. "Maddy, please wake up."

She looked at me then, though I could not tell if she saw me or if she was looking through me. Her lips pursed and a sound came out that was half a whistle, half a question. "Whooo . . . ?"

"It's Easton," I said, though I wasn't sure if she was speaking to me or if this was something from her dream. She took another step forward. I took hold of her arm and almost dropped it. Her skin was no warmer than the air itself, and if she had not been so obviously alive, I would have thought that I touched a corpse. Probably that meant that I spoke more harshly than I meant to. "Madeline!"

She stumbled. I clutched at her to keep her upright, feeling her skin too loose under my fingers. Oh God, was I leaving bruises?

I looked down at my hand on her arm and suffered another shock.

How often does anyone really think of the fine hair on a woman's arms? It hardly ever comes up. I suppose women who have particularly thick or dark hair there may find it troubling, but I was decades removed from such concerns and my sisters certainly never spoke of it. And on very old people, it seems like the hair simply goes away.

Madeline's was bright white, the color of the hair on her head, with the same drifting, floating quality. Her skin looked almost pink by comparison. My hand seemed impossibly tan and the white filaments swirled over it like some kind of pale water weed.

"Come on," I said, trying to hide my horror. "Come on, let's get you back to your room. It's too cold to be out." I looked down and saw that she was barefoot. My own slippers were inadequate to the chill radiating off the stone stairs; I couldn't imagine how cold her feet must be. I'd have picked her up and carried her, but I was afraid that I'd do her more injury than good. "Come on, Maddy."

She breathed out something, almost a word, but I could not make it out. Then her eyes rolled in the candle flame and I thought she might collapse. I tried to catch her in my free hand, but she straightened and said, "Roderick?"

"No, it's Easton."

"Oh . . ." She blinked up at me, her eyes huge in the light of the candle. "Oh, yes. Of course. Hello, Alex." She lifted one birdlike hand to her face.

"You were sleepwalking."

"Was I?" She looked around. "I . . . yes, of course, I must have been dreaming."

"Shall I take you back to your rooms?"

She looked down the stairs. "That's not necessary."

"Please," I said. "For my peace of mind. It's cold and I'll stay up all night thinking you've frozen solid and they'll find you in the morning looking like one of the Elgin Marbles."

She laughed a little, as I had intended. "Not one of the ones without a head, I hope."

"If you fall down the stairs and your head shatters, I shan't be held responsible. Come on." I tucked my arm through hers and tugged her gently back up the steps.

She followed reluctantly, still glancing over her shoulder at the stairs. "Really, Alex, I'm fine. I'm sorry to have disturbed you."

I caught her gaze and there was something odd and furtive about her expression. I drew her arm a little more firmly through mine, seized with a wild notion that she might suddenly bolt. But I saw her to the door of her room and she kept step beside me.

"Your maid should be warned that you sleepwalk," I said, as I released her.

"My maid . . . yes . . ." She drifted through the doorway into the dark. My own feet and heart were heavier as I made my own way back.

I found I could not sleep. The air seemed suddenly close and stifling, for all its chill. I pictured the hangings around the bed like great mushroom gills, dripping unseen spores down onto my face. *Urgh.* No wonder Maddy went sleepwalking.

I twitched the bed-curtain aside and grabbed for my dressing gown. Perhaps some fresh air would help. Miss Potter had helpfully explained that there were fungal spores everywhere in the air, but if I didn't have to see them, I could ignore them.

I opened the door and made my way to the balcony at the end of the hall, overlooking the lake.

The lake was full of reflected stars. The strange water gave them a faint green tinge, flickering slightly as I watched, probably from ripples. Not that the ghastly lake ever seemed to ripple when I watched. I looked up, away from the water, hoping to find an anchor in the familiar constellations.

There were no stars.

I believe I stared for at least half a minute, while this knowledge worked slowly through my brain. It was an overcast night. The sky was dark gray with a sliver of moon just edging through.

I looked back down, at a lake full of stars.

Once, on a ship in the Mediterranean, I saw the sea glow with a thousand motes of blue light. Plankton, the first mate told me. Bioluminescent plankton. After he walked away, one of the sailors said, "Don't listen to him, sir. The dead carry lanterns down in the deep."

The light in the lake was akin to that light in the sea, though more green than blue. Hundreds of individual glowing dots with no discernable source. Glowing plankton? Did that happen in lakes? I had no idea. Perhaps Miss Potter would know.

I gripped the edge of the balustrade. As I watched, I began to make out a pattern in the lights. The faint flicker was a sequence, not merely the motion of the water. A dot would brighten and then fade, and then the one next to it would do the same, giving the appearance of a light jumping along a track. Then it would begin again at the beginning.

The lights seemed to outline multiple flat, irregular sheets standing on edge in the water. I leaned forward, peering into the depths, and it seemed like there might actually be something there, something that reflected the light just a hair differently than the rest of the water, although it would have been a transparent substance. Sheets of glass? Or gelatin? Whatever made some parts of the water's surface appear matte during the day?

The moon edged out from behind the cloud, but the lights did not halt. If anything, they grew brighter and more frenzied. *Algae,* Miss Potter had said dismissively. Did algae have leaves made of jelly and outlined in light?

The lights on the Mediterranean had been beautiful. Perhaps if I had seen these on a ship, I would have found them beautiful as well. But in this dark, miserable lake, in this grim, blighted land, it was just one more unpleasantness. Perhaps this was even the source of Madeline's ailment. She had put her feet in the lake and God knew what kind of poison such things exuded into the water around them.

I turned away. Behind me, the lake continued to pulse and dance under the worried sliver of moon.

CHAPTER 6

The next day was good. I say this because it stands out so starkly alongside all the rest. The house was still damp and dark and falling down around us, Maddy and Roderick still looked like a pair of corpses headed for the bier, Denton still didn't know whether to stand up when I entered the room or not, but still . . . it was good. Roderick played the piano and we sang badly together. Maddy's voice was barely a thread and I can just about belt out the chorus to "Gallacia Will Go On" if somebody else handles everything past the first verse. Denton didn't know most of our songs, and we knew none of his. But none of that particularly mattered. He sang something about John Brown's body, and I picked up enough to bellow, "Glory, glory, hallelujah!" at the appropriate moments.

Roderick was a genius on the piano, though. When we had exhausted ourselves mangling popular tunes, he played dramatic compositions by great composers. (Mozart? Beethoven? Why are you asking me? It was music, it went dun-dun-dun-DUN, what more do you want me to say?)

It was *fun*. People get hung up on happiness and joy, but fun will take you at least as far and it's generally cheaper to obtain. We had fun. Maddy laughed and clapped her hands and there was color in her cheeks. I hoped like hell that the beef had been having some effect, even if the cook had to use mortar fire to tenderize the beast.

Maddy went to bed and I broke out a bottle of livrit. Livrit is a Gallacian specialty, which means it's uniquely terrible. It strongly resembles vodka, although vodka would be ashamed to acknowledge the connection, sweetened, as livrit is, with the cloudberries that grow in the mountains. That might actually be palatable, though, and we can't have that, so lichen is also included. The resulting drink starts syrupy, ends bitter, and burns all the way down. No one actually likes it, but it is traditionally made by widows as a means of supporting themselves, so everyone drinks it because you can't let little old ladies starve to death when they could be climbing mountains and scraping lichen off rocks instead.

Every Gallacian soldier I know carries at least one bottle of livrit with kan. It reminds us that we are part of a great and glorious tradition of people doing gallant things in the service of a country that can't find its arse with both hands and a map. Being as I was an officer, I carry three, in case I run into some poor sod who's drunk kan only bottle.

We toasted Gallacia and Ruravia, and Denton gagged and Roderick and I cheered on this completely normal response to livrit. Then we toasted America and the taste buds her son had lost that day. Then we toasted a couple more things, including Maddy's beauty, fallen comrades, and the foolishness of armies.

And then we parted and went to bed, and that was the last remotely normal day in the house of Usher.

I was just sitting down on the bed to pull off my boots when I heard the creak of floorboards outside my room. Was it truly that late? We'd been carousing for a few hours, long enough that Maddy might have begun sleepwalking again. I shoved my foot back in the boot and threw open the door.

"Oh," I said, startled. "It's you."

Denton looked at me in mild surprise. "You were expecting someone else?"

"I thought you might be Madeline." Belatedly it occurred to me how that must sound, as if I was expecting Maddy to visit my rooms in the night. "I found her sleepwalking the other night."

"Really." Denton frowned. "I had not known that she did that. Roderick said something about her walking the halls, but I thought . . ."

"I know," I said, closing my door behind me. "She doesn't seem well enough to walk much of anywhere without help. I was afraid she would faint or fall down."

"Did you wake her?"

"I did. I know you're not supposed to wake a sleepwalker, but she thanked me. Said she'd been dreaming."

"This place breeds nightmares," said Denton, with unexpected savagery. "I need some air."

"I'll join you," I said. The livrit was burning off and I had no desire to sober up in the closeness of my room. The balcony overlooking the lake had little appeal, but it was at the back of my mind that perhaps Denton would see the strange lights, too. "I haven't been sleeping well myself."

Once we were outside in the open air, I asked, "What did you mean, this place breeds nightmares?"

"Roderick," said Denton, leaning against the stone railing. "He complains of nightmares. Says the walls breathe them out."

I did not know about the walls, but I could definitely imagine the lake doing so. No matter how innocent the water looked right now, I could not shake the memory of those strange, transparent sheets and the outlines of rippling light.

"Have you had any?" It was not a question I would normally ask someone that I knew as little as I knew Denton, but there are things that two old soldiers can talk about in the dark after drinking that ka would never discuss in daylight.

"I had a nightmare last night," said Denton, not looking at me. The lake reflected the stars back, dark and still. "I was back in the surgical tent, amputating. After a battle . . . the way the rifle bullets shattered limbs . . . we would take off dozens in a day. One of the orderlies would carry them away, but we had to move so fast, before the men bled out, so they would end up outside the tent, in a pile. I was looking at the pile, and there were so many severed limbs, but they were alive. They were moving."

"Good God," I said, horrified.

"They were still alive, and I realized we shouldn't have cut them off. If I could just take them back to their owners, I could put them back. I could make those men whole again. But there were so many, and there was a crowd of soldiers begging me to help them, and I didn't know which leg or arm went with which person and there were so many men, and I couldn't help any of them. . . ."

His voice trailed off. I shuddered. "I'm sorry," I said.

"I don't dream about the war much anymore," he said. "It was a long time ago. A lot longer for me than yours was for you, I imagine. But you won't always dream of it. If you're worried."

I nodded. I certainly wasn't going to bother to deny it. I had been good at being a soldier. Better than I had been at being anything else. And I had always thought that if you were going to have stupid bloody wars, it was better to have people who were good at it doing the fighting. People who knew what to expect and when to dive for cover and when to run. People who knew what it looked like when their buddy took a bullet and could staunch the bleeding instead of standing around with their mouths hanging open.

But there's a price you pay for being good at some things. The war is the backdrop to most of my dreams. The house I grew up in, my grandmother's cottage, and the war, as if it was a place that I lived. I can't even say they're all nightmares. Sometimes it's just where the dream is happening.

Denton knew. Roderick might. I don't know. He had always been jumpy. Nothing wrong with that. Jumpy means you survive. It also means you wear yourself out faster and drive the rest of your unit nuts, but everybody copes in their own way. He was never going to be a career soldier, but that's fine. Not everyone should be. Ideally nobody would have to be, but that's a bigger problem than I could tackle today.

I looked down into the still water. No glow tonight. I wondered if I could convince myself it had been a dream. *This place breeds nightmares.*

No. I knew what I had seen. I am not a particularly

fanciful person. (A Frenchwoman once told me that I had no poetry in my soul. I recited a dirty limerick to her, and she threw a lemon at my head. Paris is a marvelous city.) If I was no longer able to distinguish between dreams and waking then something was wrong with me, as well as with the Ushers.

"What do you think of this lake?" I asked Denton abruptly.

"It's a dismal thing," said Denton. If he was surprised by my change of topic, he didn't say anything. "You'd think a pristine mountain lake would be picturesque."

"The ones in Gallacia are."

"I only popped over the border once, I think. Place with the turnips on the shutters, right?"

I muttered something in defense of the turnips and stared into the water. "It's like it doesn't reflect right."

"The lake?" Denton leaned forward over the balustrade and gazed down. "Possibly. Or what it's reflecting is so depressing that it doesn't help. I don't know. Reminds me of some of the springs we have in the States. Fantastic colors from the minerals leached into it, and it'll kill you dead if you drink from it." He straightened up. "Though I suppose it would have done so by now, since I imagine it's where all the water's drawn from."

I grimaced. I hadn't given that any thought. If something in the tarn was poisoning Madeline, it was in all our veins now. I felt vaguely queasy, even though I knew it was my imagination. "I thought I saw lights in it, the other night."

"Lights?" He looked over at me, surprised. I wished I hadn't said anything. Clearly the livrit had loosened my tongue.

"Like reflections of the stars. Only it was overcast and there weren't any stars to be had. I don't know. And once I looked at them, they seemed to pulse. Reminded me of the lights you get in the sea sometimes." I was downplaying it tremendously, but it sounded completely mad when I said it aloud. I should have spoken to Miss Potter first, and gotten some scientific words to use as a talisman. "The English-woman that's been roaming around painting mushrooms thinks there's some kind of algae in the water."

"Huh." Denton looked down into the water. "It doesn't surprise me, I suppose. Any damn thing could grow in that lake, and it wouldn't surprise me."

I joined him in gazing down over the edge. It was dark and still and silent.

"Madeline nearly drowned in that lake a few months ago," said Denton absently.

"What?!"

"Roderick didn't tell you?" For a moment he looked as if he, too, wished he hadn't said anything. Then he shrugged. "She claims she doesn't remember. Had an episode and fell in. Roderick was certain she'd drowned when he pulled her out, but ironically, the catalepsy may have saved her. She didn't draw any water into her lungs, you see."

"Christ's blood." I remembered the white shape of Made-line on the shore of the lake. Why was she still visiting the thing alone? I should speak to her about it. Though surely she must be aware of the dangers.

I was caught up in my thoughts and almost missed a greenish flicker in the depths. "There! Did you catch that?"

"I saw something . . . there it is again! Be damned." Den-ton leaned so far over the railing that I thought I might have to grab him and pull him back. "Huh."

We both gazed into the water for a long time, but there were no more lights to be seen. Eventually we parted ways and went back to our respective beds. I don't know how Denton fared, but for me, sleep was still a long time coming.

It was early morning when I heard the floorboards creak again. Christ, the bloody things were better than doorbells. This time the steps were halting and slow and I knew it wasn't Denton.

I had actually managed to sleep a few hours, and I am ashamed to admit that for a moment I thought of simply ignoring the sounds and going back to sleep. Livrit has a bite like a distempered mule, even if you're used to it. But chivalry demanded that I get up, because those light, tentative footsteps could only have been Maddy.

She had left the hall by the time I had pulled on my dressing gown, but it did not matter. I had a fairly good idea where she was going. I caught up to her halfway down the stairs.

Her walk was stiff and strange, starting and stopping the movements at odd places. It put me in mind of something, though I couldn't think of what. More importantly, it meant that she was slow on the steps, and my stomach clenched at how easy it would be for her to fall.

"Madeline, you're sleepwalking again."

She turned to look at me, her eyes again bright but unfocused. "Whooooo?" she breathed.

"It's me. Easton. Remember?"

Madeline swung her head from side to side. It didn't look like she was shaking her head, exactly. Her whole neck moved. I was reminded of the way that Hob swings his head to shake off flies. "Tooo . . . 'annnyyy . . ." Another odd swinging motion.

Too any?

Realization dawned. *Too many.* Her lips moved as if they were stiff, and the "M" sound was barely there, while the rest were drawn out. Too many. Too many what?

"Whooo?" She stretched a hand toward me, pointing.

Too many words? I tried to simplify. "Easton. Eeeast-uhn."

Madeline seemed to relax, as if I had finally grasped what she was asking. "Eeeestun."

"Yes. That's right." Was it the catalepsy? Denton had said that she became paralyzed to the point of coma, but was this another symptom? Were her lips and perhaps the joint at the top of the neck unable to move? Could she not focus her eyes and see who I was? Or was she still sleepwalking, and this was all a symptom of the dream? I took her arm in case she might fall. I barely dared to touch the skin, but I could feel the fine, dead white hair tickling against my palm.

"One," she said. "Two . . . thhhhreee . . . 'our . . . 'ive . . . sixsss . . ." She paused as if thinking. "Se'en . . . eight . . . nnnine . . . te-uhn." She looked at me. "Gooood?"

"Very good," I said, wondering what the hell was going on.

She nodded, throwing her head up and down as violently as a horse fighting a bit. "Hhharrd," she said. "Vreath 'ooving hhharrd."

Breath moving hard, I translated internally, after a moment of puzzlement. Was she saying it was hard to breathe? Had she been counting breaths?

Then she smiled and it was terrible.

Madeline's lips pulled up at the corners in a terrible parody of good humor, her mouth stretching painfully wide, her jaw dropped so far that it looked almost like a scream. Above that awful grin, her eyes were as flat and dead as stones.

I do not delude myself that I have seen every way the

human mind can fail, though I have seen a hundred ways that soldiers and civilians can break in war. But I had never seen a smile like that.

I stumbled backward, dropping her arm. There was the faintest of ripping sensations against my fingers. It was so unexpected that I looked down and saw my hand covered in the fine white hair from her arms. Dear God, had I closed my hand and pulled it out by the roots?

No. When I looked in horror at her forearm, there was a handprint of bare flesh left behind. Each finger was visible, and the outline of my thumb against her wrist, but I had not left a bruise. Had it been so shallowly rooted in the skin that my merest touch had torn it free?

The new horror replaced the old. I looked up and she no longer wore that horrible grin. "Oh, Maddy . . ." I said miserably, trying to wipe the hair off on my trousers. It stuck to my sweating palms like cat hair.

She shook her head again. "No 'Addy."

"What?"

"*No Maddy.*" She was clearly trying to enunciate, even though the "M" came out more like "Uh-addy." She banged her wrist against her sternum and I winced, expecting even that light pressure to leave bruises.

"No?" What on earth was she dreaming about?

Another flailing nod. "One," she said. "Maddy *one.* Meee *one.* Maddy . . . Meee . . . *two.*"

"Two," I agreed.

She seemed to sag. "Vreath 'ooving hharrd," she muttered. I did not know whether to try to steady her or to avoid touching her again.

"You must be tired," I said sympathetically.

"Tiiirrd," she agreed.

"Let's go back to your room," I suggested. I took her shoulders, where the cloth covered them, reluctant to touch her bare skin again for fear of tearing more hair loose. "This way."

Maddy allowed me to steer her back to her room. She pointed to things as we passed and named each one, like a small child learning to speak. "Waall. Stair. Cannndle. Eaaastonn."

No maid greeted us when I pushed open the door to her room. Damnation. I led her to the bed, wondering how to get her to lie down without panicking her or leaving even more bruises. "Down," I said, as if she were a dog. "Let's lie down."

"Dowwwuhn," she agreed. The bed was a mess. I saw more hair everywhere on the sheets, as if she'd been shedding. Christ's blood. It's never a good sign when people's hair falls out. I would have to tell Denton.

Unfortunately, once I'd gotten Maddy into bed, I realized that I had no idea which room was his. There were a hundred doors in this great hulk. I could go about yelling, I supposed, but what was Denton going to do tonight that he wouldn't do in daylight?

I was halfway back to my room before I realized what Maddy's stilted walk had reminded me of.

It was the hare.

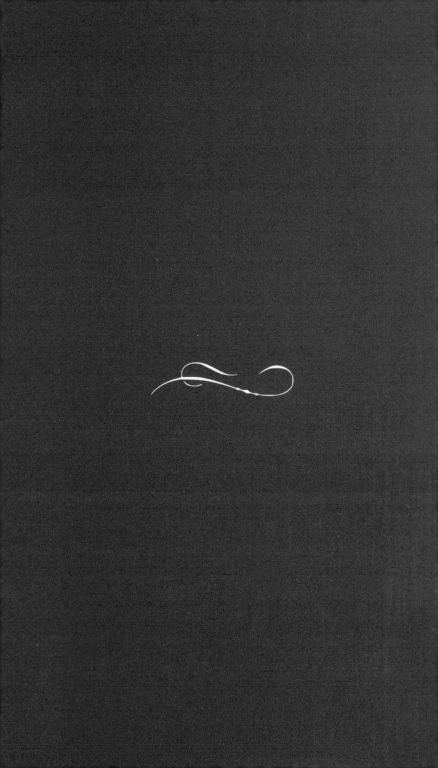

CHAPTER 7

I found Roderick at breakfast before Denton. "Have you seen Maddy today?" I asked. "She was sleepwalking again last night. And she seemed very confused. She didn't know me, and she couldn't talk very well." I decided not to mention that terrible smile, or the way that her stiff walk had reminded me of the strange crawling hare.

"That happens sometimes," said Roderick, staring at his plate.

"Can't her maid keep her from walking?"

"Her maid died three months ago."

This rocked me back. No maid. Of course they wouldn't have money to hire a new one. I was an ass. I tried again. "Her hair is falling out. She's . . . shedding. It's terrible."

"Her hair. Yes." Roderick nodded. After a moment he added, "That's been happening. The servants try to clean it up, but . . ."

"Roderick . . ." The defeat in his voice infuriated me.

Couldn't he see that his sister was dying? "You have to do something!"

"Do *what*?" He slammed his fist down on the sideboard with sudden rage. "Don't you think I know? Don't you think I'd fix it if I could? Take her to Paris—blow up this damned house—fill in that accursed lake—"

I blinked at him. Part of me said that blowing up the house was not actually a solution to Madeline's problems, but another part was already calculating how much dynamite would be required.

He must have read my expression because he sagged in his chair, his rage gone as quickly as it had come. "Don't tempt me, Easton. I already know where I'd put the match."

"I believe the lieutenant actually meant that you should get another doctor," said Denton from the doorway. He nodded to me. "Morning, Easton."

"That's not exactly what I meant," I said, even though the thought of calling a specialist in from Paris had crossed my mind.

"I don't know why not," said Denton. "I can't have impressed you with my depth of knowledge of her case." He didn't seem particularly offended.

"You know more about it than I do, certainly. Have you seen how her hair is falling out?"

"I have." He glared at his cup of tea. "Not surprising in a severe illness. Now ask me how she still has any hair left to shed."

I paused with my tea halfway to my lips.

"I don't know," he said, answering the question anyway. "No goddamn idea. If it's falling out like that, it shouldn't be regrowing, but it is."

"Coming in stark white, too," I said.

"Yes. The closest I can guess is that it's not growing so much as the follicles and the skin receding, the same way that people grow hair after they've die—" He cut himself off and applied himself savagely to his breakfast.

"No one else," said Roderick. "No more doctors. This has all gone much further than it should have already. I do not want Madeline poked and prodded like . . . like some kind of animal in a cage." His sudden animation seemed to have fled. He leaned against the sideboard, swaying as if exhausted.

I bowed my head, made my excuses, and headed for the stables.

"This is all a mess, boy," I told Hob.

His ears indicated that he agreed, particularly since he was not being given a treat. Speaking of, I dug an apple out of a nearby saddlebag. There had been large orchards farther down the mountain and I had purchased several bags, then forgotten about them. Hob, it seemed, had not.

"I'm starting to wonder if there really is something in the water. Something fatal."

Hob expressed that lack of apples might prove equally fatal.

"Denton doesn't know. I don't know who else to ask." The doctor's gelding put his nose over the stall door and, though he offered no useful advice, I held an apple out to him as well. Satisfied equine crunching noises followed me as I went looking for Usher's library.

Every manor house has one, of course. I don't know what I really expected to do there—it's not as if I am a terribly keen reader, and I knew even then that a medical textbook would probably be beyond my ability, particularly in another language. I speak quite good Ruravian, French, and

English, and I can manage to get by in German (mostly because Germans always instantly switch to another language, which they inevitably speak better than you do, and politely ask you to practice it with them). But reading in those languages is something else again, particularly when it's technical. Still, I had to try. I had some idea in my head that there might be a disease among the hares that had also affected Maddy. If not a disease, perhaps a parasite. Undercooked pork and the like can sicken a human, so why not something in a hare?

The problem, of course, was that I had only a hunter's notion of what the inside of a hare is supposed to look like, so if it was anything more subtle than "there is a large squirmy bit where a large squirmy bit does not belong," I could not tell merely by shooting a hare and dissecting it. Hence the library.

Rows of leather bindings stared down at me from high shelves. There was no fire laid in the grate and the cold, creeping damp hung in the air like fog.

Looking up at all those bindings, my heart sank. What was I even looking for? A book that said, "The Anatomy Of The European Hare, With Clearly Labeled Diagrams For The Novice" perhaps? Did they even make books like that?

"Well, they ought to," I grumbled to myself. "It'd be more useful than half the books that get written these days. How many works on the life of Lord Byron does the world really need, anyway?" I pulled down a book at random and opened it.

Tried to open it.

The swollen pages stuck together. I fitted my fingernail between two of them and managed to pry them apart, only to rip one in half and leave most of it stuck to the opposite page. The book wasn't just damp, it had been soggy for so long that it had practically turned to mush.

I groaned and pulled down another book. This one's pages were wavy from having swollen and dried and swollen and dried, and while it opened, there was a line of mold all around the edge, so dark that it could almost have been mistaken for a decorative border.

"Christ's blood," I muttered to myself.

"Ah," said Roderick from the doorway. "You have found the great library. Pride of generations of Ushers." He must have seen my expression, because his lips twisted into a humorless smile. "Don't worry, my father sold all the rare books already. We didn't lose anything much."

"Are they all like this?" I asked, gazing up at the bookshelves with their burden of rotting words.

"Every last one. The servants dry out some of them to use as tinder now and again. They'll burn if you get them hot enough." His gaze swept across the shelves, as if picturing them in flame.

I did not know what to say. How do you express sympathy for a man's manor house gone to ruin? I struggled for a joke instead. "Should have stayed in Gallacia, Roderick. Then you could have gone to the royal lending library and checked out a book."

"We should have all stayed in Gallacia," he said, not bothering with my attempt at humor. "My mother was right."

"Bah, you can both come stay with me," I said. "Admittedly I only own one very small former hunting lodge and we'd be living in each other's pockets, but it's a snug little place."

Roderick shook his head. "She won't leave," he repeated. "And I . . ." He looked around the room, a man gazing on the face of his enemy. "I begin to think that this place has killed all of us, in its time. Perhaps it's too late for me as well."

"It's only a building, Roderick."

"Is it?" He turned away. "I hear the woodworms gnawing in the beams," he muttered. "Would to God that they would gnaw a little faster."

I can't say this discussion put me in a particularly hopeful frame of mind. I left the library myself and went looking for Denton.

"Hello," he said, looking up from a book that he was reading (which, presumably, he had brought with him). "You have a singularly focused look about you."

"What do you know about hares?" I asked.

He blinked at me. "Come again?"

"Hares. The animal. Long ears. Hops around. Boxes in springtime."

"You mean rabbits?"

Christ save me from Americans. "No, they're bigger. You don't have hares?"

He had to think about it. "Err . . . wait, I think they've got them up north. Snowshoe hares, they call them. Why?"

"Is it possible there could be a disease in the hares that might have affected Madeline? Something that she could catch from them somehow?"

"I don't know of any."

"But is it possible? Something that could afflict both hare and human?"

"Of course it's possible. Rabies affects them both. But I trust you're not suggesting that Madeline has rabies?"

"No, no." I sank down in the chair. "The hares around here act strange. All the locals say they're possessed. No, I don't believe that." I raised a hand to forestall Denton's protests. "Most of us go to the Devil without him having to personally oversee things. But I saw a hare out on the moors that moved very strangely, and Maddy sleepwalking reminded me of it. . . ."

It sounded ridiculous when I said it out loud. I was grasping at straws and I knew it. But to his credit, Denton was apparently willing to grasp those straws alongside me. "You think there's some connection?"

"Possibly? Maddy was never sickly. But Roderick doesn't have it, so I thought it couldn't just be some miasma in the air or the water. . . ."

"The servants would have mentioned if there was some similar disease in the village."

"Yes, of course." I sighed. The mention of the servants reminded me, though—"Madeline's maid. Do you know what she died of?"

"She threw herself off the roof."

I stared at him.

"This is not a good house for anyone," he said, "but certainly not for those of melancholic temper."

"Christ's blood."

Denton took pity on me, or perhaps it was just his way of holding on to that straw. "It's still not a bad notion. There are diseases that only affect a very few people. Leprosy, for example. The vast majority of us are immune, except for the poor devils who aren't."

I nodded eagerly. "So Maddy could be susceptible. The problem is that if I shoot a hare, I realize that I have no way of telling whether it's normal unless there's something really extraordinarily wrong. Would you be able to tell?"

"I'm not a veterinarian," he said. "Or a cook. But I suppose I could take a look at one and see if anything jumps out at me."

I nodded. "Then tomorrow I'll see if I can fetch you a hare."

In the end it was Hob who located the hare, by virtue of nearly stepping on it. He spotted it at the last moment, snorted, and pulled sideways, hopping on three hooves. I was rather startled myself, particularly when the hare didn't move. It just sat there, staring up at the pair of us with its wild, empty eyes.

"Go on," I told the hare. "Walk a bit." It would do me no good to shoot a hare that wasn't afflicted by this nameless malady.

It did not oblige. I slid off Hob's back and took out the gun I used on small game (not cows). "Come on, scoot."

The hare stared at me. I took a step forward, then another. Christ, was I going to have to actually nudge the thing with my boot?

Before I touched it, it turned and began that strange crawling walk. It moved more rapidly than I would have expected. I took aim, only to watch it vanish into a stubby copse of trees, which were either dead or doing a remarkable imitation of it.

"My own fault for being slow," I muttered. "Hob, stay." I ground tied him and went after the hare.

The dead trees did not improve upon close inspection. I stepped inside the copse, looking for the hare, and found it sitting up, watching me.

"Right," I said. "You've definitely got it, whatever it is." I started to sight down the barrel, although I could probably have bashed it over the head with the butt of my gun just as easily.

Movement in the corner of my eye distracted me. I turned my head and saw another hare, moving in the same unpleasant fashion. It looked almost spidery somehow. I had the sudden absurd notion of a disembodied hand walking along on its fingers, or of living limbs separated from their owners. Clearly Denton's dream had lodged itself in my brain.

I turned back to the original, only to find that a third had joined it. All three of them stood up on their hind legs, watching me.

The hairs on the back of my neck stood to attention.

I shot one of them. It might have been the first of them, but they might also have been changing places. A child could not have missed at that range. The copse rang with the shot and the hare collapsed.

None of the other hares moved. They did not even flinch.

A wave of tinnitus struck in the wake of the gunshot, and as I waited for the ringing to subside, I realized that there could be even more hares behind me now and I would not hear them approaching.

Which meant nothing, I told myself. (I hate how the tinnitus seems to drown out my thoughts as well, so that I feel as if I'm shouting inside my own skull.) They were hares, not wolves. A hare might give you a nasty bite if you grabbed it, but it wasn't going to go for your throat.

I knew all this, and yet every instinct I had began to scream that something was behind me. Something dangerous. Something that was not a hare.

I do not argue with my instincts. They kept me alive in the war. I spun around to find two more hares sitting at the edge of the copse, watching.

My hearing began to slowly return to normal, but the skin-crawling sensation that Something Else was there did not subside. I turned again, and the original three hares were now four, as if another had sprung up from the ground like a mushroom.

"Right," I said. I stomped forward and snatched up the dead hare. "That's tha—"

It moved in my hand.

I flung it violently away, even knowing that it was a convulsion, that many animals kick after being killed. I had shot it in the head, it could not possibly be alive. Muscles spasm, that's all.

I was cursing myself for a fool when the dead hare began to crawl away.

It did not try to escape. That was somehow the most horrible part of all. It crawled back to its position in the circle of hares and it sat up, despite half its skull being missing. It turned its head so that its remaining eye pointed at me and tucked its paws against its chest like all the others.

Whatever looked out at me through that eye was not a hare.

My nerve broke and I ran.

Perhaps if I was less skeptical and more credulous, I might have fared better. At the time, all I could think was that I could not possibly have seen what I thought I saw. The dead did not get up and walk around.

Sometimes, however, the *nearly* dead do. I have seen men with terrible injuries run a hundred yards to fall upon the enemy. I have seen men with bullets lodged in their skulls continue to fight, sometimes for days. Hell, Partridge, who was under my command, thought ka was merely hit in the head until a doctor found the bullet hole almost a week later. Fortunately he had the good sense not to try to remove it. So far as I knew, Partridge was still alive, although ka complained that ever since the bullet, ka'd had no sense of taste.

It was possible that the hare had been like Partridge. Perhaps my shot hadn't been true. Perhaps when I thought that it was missing part of its head, it was simply bloody fur falling down in a particularly grotesque formation. The hares were the same dull gray-brown as the sedges, were they not? My eyes might have been playing tricks on me. And Christ knew that I had been jumpy and my nerves had been playing up. No, I was not a reliable observer.

I recast it in my head, trying to make an amusingly self-deprecating tale of it, and eventually related it to Denton. "The damn things all stared at me and I had a fit of nerves and ran away from a pack of animals that wouldn't come up to the top of my boots. Can you believe it? Chest full of medals for valor under fire, and I squawked like a chicken because I flubbed the shot and the damn thing kicked in my hand." I forced a rueful grin. "Between that and the cow, I'm not showing up well in the gunnery department."

Denton, despite my best attempts at a diverting tale, was not diverted. He draped his hands over his knees, a line forming between his thick eyebrows. "That is most unsettling."

"For the pride of Gallacia, certainly."

"Not that." He frowned. "Roderick says that you are not particularly fanciful."

"I like to think that, though you wouldn't know it from this afternoon." I shrugged. "Well, you know as well as I do. Sometimes the oddest things set off our nerves."

"True enough," Denton admitted. "Soldier's heart, we called it after the war. I once had a bit of an episode because they had lined the street with flags, and the wind came up and they were all snapping . . . the sound wasn't like cannon fire at all, but it still was, you know?"

I nodded. I did indeed know.

"Then one of the flags came loose and it blew toward me." He snorted. "Found myself down a stairwell two streets over." His voice had that light veneer of humor that we all get, because if we don't pretend we're laughing, we might have to admit just how broken we are. It's like telling stories at the bar about the worst pain you've ever been in. You laugh and you brag about it, and it turns the pain into something that will buy you a drink.

"There, you see?" I waved a hand airily. "*Névrose de guerre,* the French call it. Makes it sound like a bloody pastry. Though I do feel bad that I flubbed the shot. I should have stayed to finish it off. Hopefully a fox or a falcon or something will take it before too long."

Denton's humor faded. He took a large swallow of the drink beside him. "Perhaps you didn't flub the shot," he said, not looking at me.

"Of course I did. It got up and walked away." I didn't tell him about it sitting up and watching me. That went well beyond *névrose de guerre.*

He said nothing.

"The dead don't walk," I said, hearing my voice rise angrily. "You of all people should know that."

Denton looked at me for a long, long moment, searching my face for something. He must not have found it, because he looked away and said, "Ignore me. I'm becoming as fanciful as Roderick. I don't know what I know anymore."

I stalked away and took my dinner in my room that night. Angus watched me angle the chair so that my back was against the wall and said nothing at all.

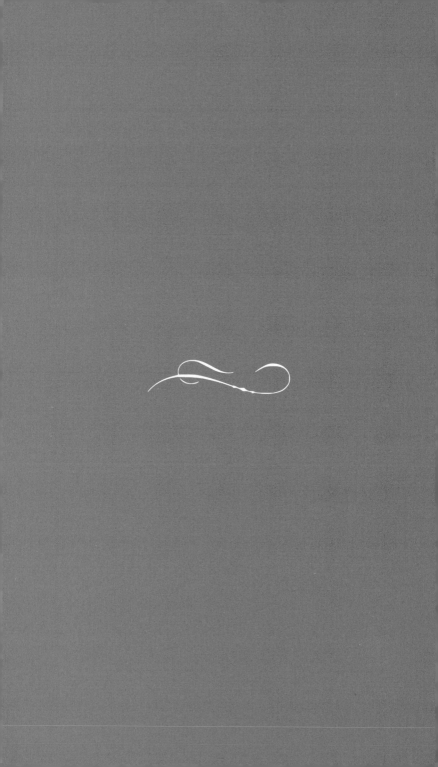

CHAPTER 8

Ironically, I dropped off to sleep instantly that night. Perhaps it was because all the tensions were too close to the surface again. Falling asleep quickly, whenever you have the chance, is the third thing you learn in the army. (The first thing you learn is to keep your mouth shut and let the sergeants blunt their teeth on the people who can't. The second thing is to never pass up a chance to piss.)

I woke only once, when I fancied I heard a cry. It sounded like a male voice, deep and hoarse. I bolted upright in bed, grabbing for my pistol, but did not hear anything else.

Battle nerves, I told myself. After the day I'd had, perhaps it was no wonder. I listened carefully, and just as I was thinking of getting up and prowling about, I heard Angus snore from the next room. I'm used to the sounds that Angus makes, of course, but his snore is quite legendary and it's entirely possible that it might have worked its way into a nightmare and woken me. I put the pistol back down on the night table and went back to sleep.

I woke the second time to music.

It was a glorious, layered composition, half a dirge and half a joyous melody, the notes weaving and intertwining like the flight of mating birds. I knew at once that it was Roderick. No one else in the house played at all, and I doubt many people on earth play like *that*. The notes Roderick coaxed from that piano were so far beyond my meager ability to comprehend that I can barely explain it to you. It was like sipping a fine vintage wine and knowing that there were complexities that you would never be able to taste, hidden depths that you could not understand. Roderick's music was genius, and I knew just enough to know that I could not appreciate just how far beyond me it truly was. I followed the music to the conservatory and leaned in the doorway, soaked it up.

When he finished at last, with a trailing set of notes that sounded more like a flute than a piano, I broke into applause. "Bravo! Bravo!"

Roderick let out a shriek and jumped halfway off the piano bench, clutching his chest. I cursed myself for having overset his nerves again. "Sorry! I'm sorry, old man, I didn't mean to startle you. I didn't want to interrupt, that's all."

"No. No, it's all right." He sagged back down on the bench. "I mean, it's not all right, but it's not your fault. Oh hell."

I edged into the room. "Are you all right?"

"Madeline is dead," he said.

I stared at him. I knew the words that he was saying, and they were in my own language, but I kept trying to parse them as something else, something that merely sounded similar. Maddy couldn't be dead. She had been alive two days ago.

I had spoken to her in the hall. We had sung songs around the piano. "I . . . are you sure?"

It was a foolish question. Of course he was sure. He loved his sister to the point of exiling himself in this miserable heap. But death is when you are allowed to ask foolish questions and to say all the unforgivable things that will be immediately forgiven.

"I'm sure," he said. "Denton checked. She had one of her fits. She stopped breathing." He stared down at the keys and touched one hesitantly, as if he had forgotten how to play.

"Roderick, I'm sorry." I came into the room and thumped him on the back and did all the things that soldiers do with each other because most of us have forgotten how to cry.

"It was terrible," he said softly. "I never wanted . . ."

"I know."

"I've known I'd have to, but . . ."

"I know, Roderick. I know."

He straightened and turned away, his shoulders hunched. "I heard her walking in the halls and now . . . now . . ." He shook his head violently.

I blew out my breath in a long sigh. Maddy was dead and it had been inevitable and yet it made no sense at all.

"She did not suffer," said Denton from the doorway. "Or rather, her suffering is at an end."

Part of me wanted to ask if he could have been mistaken, if the catalepsy could present the illusion of death. The other part of me knew that he was a doctor and I was just a soldier, and the death I knew was not a subtle thing. "Can I see her?" I asked instead. "Madeline?"

Denton and Roderick looked at each other. After a moment, Roderick said, "She's in the crypt."

"I see no reason why you shouldn't," said Denton firmly.

"Yes," said Roderick. "Yes, of course. I'll get a lamp."

The crypt was a long and winding way, down narrow stone steps in the back of the house. The cold damp became an active chill, and yet the air seemed somehow drier as we reached the bottom, as if we had burrowed beneath the clammy air that held the house in its grip.

"I did not realize that the crypt was beneath the house itself," I said as we walked.

"The ground here is hard to dig," said Roderick simply. "They blasted it to make the cellars. It was easier, I expect, to add the crypt as well."

"Like a church."

He grunted. The stairs down only reinforced my opinion, though, carved as they were with Gothic ornament. The old lords of Usher had no interest in simplicity.

The door itself was another one of the pointed arched doors, made of ancient wood, locked and barred. Roderick handed Denton the lamp and pulled the bar out of its sockets with a strength that belied the frailness of his arms. He set it down and we stepped inside the crypt.

Cold, it was cold. A long, rough-hewn corridor led away, presumably deeper into the crypt, but the chamber we stood in held a single stone slab, carved with crosses and a procession of mourners.

Madeline lay under a shroud, faceless and featureless. Roderick stood over her protectively, his whole body bristling. I had thought to approach more closely, to look on Maddy's face one last time, but Roderick looked so forbidding that I refrained. *Really, what good would it do? Have you not seen enough bodies in your time? Maybe it helps other people, but it's just one more face to haunt your dreams.*

I went to one knee and prayed instead. The Lord's Prayer, dredged up from some long-ago memory of church services. When I was done, Denton waited for a short moment, then touched my arm and ushered me away from the crypt and the slim white form on the slab.

It came to me, as we made our way up the steps, that anyone could have been under that shroud. I could not tell that it was Maddy. I could not tell that it was anything human at all.

Roderick was so jumpy at dinner that he very nearly set me off. He kept jerking upright and looking over his shoulder, as if an enemy was going to emerge from the paneling and go for his back. "Steady on, old fellow," I said. "You're going to have me diving under the table at this rate."

"I hear the worms," he muttered. "Soon they'll start on her. Unless they don't."

I told myself that it wasn't my sister and I had no damn business being offended. Roderick stopped jumping, but began to wring his hands together. He had pale, long-fingered hands, but the way he scrubbed them, one over the other, began to redden them. I eyed this warily, but at least it didn't make me want to dive for cover. Denton ate methodically through the food in front of him, not speaking. What he thought, I couldn't guess.

I ended up in the library after dinner, accompanied by my second bottle of livrit. It was terrible, but a hangover seemed like a great idea. Headache is always preferable to heartache, and if you're focusing on not throwing up, you aren't thinking about how the friends of your youth are dying around you.

I didn't know why Maddy's death hit me so hard. I saw the Ushers a few times a season growing up, that was all. I could not say with any honesty that I thought of them often, before receiving Maddy's letter.

Perhaps this miserable place had weighed down my spirit and left me vulnerable. Perhaps it was simply that she was the first person my age to die of illness, instead of in the jagged teeth of the war.

I slugged back the livrit straight from the bottle. My throat no longer burned, but the syrupy taste still made the hinge of my jaw ache. The room stank of moldy leather and the death of books, but I could no longer smell anything but livrit.

Angus found me eventually. He stoppered the bottle and pried me out of the chair. "Come on, child," he said, "I'm too old to carry you. Feet forward."

I muttered something about letting me lie on the floor with my booze and my grief.

"*March!*" Angus barked, and my hindbrain took over, pointed me in the correct direction, and marched.

I felt like hammered shit in the morning, of course. That was the point. The thought of food was nauseating, but if I didn't eat, everything was going to be a lot worse. I splashed water on my face then braced myself on my hands, staring into the basin. Did it come from the tarn? Christ's blood. Maybe I was better off with the livrit after all.

One of the few things I learned from the Brits who served with me was that if you're feeling dreadful, it helps to dress well. I dragged on fresh clothes. My tongue felt like it needed a shave. Angus came in, looked at me, grunted, and handed me my boots, which had been freshly polished.

"Don't say it," I muttered.

He gripped my shoulder briefly, but didn't utter a word. I shoved my feet in the boots and went to breakfast.

My hand was halfway to the knob when I heard Roderick say, "I heard her knocking last night."

Denton said something, too quietly for me to hear.

"On the door of the crypt," Roderick said. "Trying to get out. It can't have been, though, can it? She's dead. She's really dead, isn't she?"

"Of course she is," I said, pushing the door open. "Your nerves are shot, and who can blame you?" I looked to Denton for confirmation.

"Yes, of course," he said. "Only nerves."

"Yes," said Roderick. "Of course. You must think me quite mad, Easton."

"Not at all. *Névrose de guerre*. We've all got it. It'd be more extraordinary if you weren't overset."

He began wringing his hands together again. His knuckles were so red that they looked as if they might start bleeding.

"For God's sake, leave off, man," I said wearily. "You're like Lady Macbeth. 'Out, out, damn'd spot!'"

Roderick let out a yelp like a kicked dog and stared at me with huge eyes. I immediately felt guilty. "Sorry, Roderick. It's . . . it's just everything." I sat back. "Why don't we leave? Go to Paris? It'd be good for you."

"No!" he cried, almost a shout. "No, I . . ." He swallowed, his throat bobbing. "No, I can't. Not until she's . . . not until . . ." His voice shrank. "Not yet," he whispered finally, and fled the table.

"Think about it," I called after him. I looked over at Denton. "I wish you'd help me convince him."

"He won't go yet," said Denton. "You should probably go, though. This is no place for decent folk."

"When do you think Roderick might be willing to travel?"

"Not for a time," he said. "Not until he's . . . ah . . . certain that his sister has been properly laid to rest."

I rested my elbows on the table and my face in my hands. "Damnable foolishness," I said. "The dead are dead. They don't care."

"They don't fear ghosts in Gallacia?" he asked. I could hear the edge of a smile in his voice, and also what that smile was costing him.

"No, we're as superstitious as anyone else," I admitted. "Someone must sit with the body for three days to make sure that wandering spirits don't take possession of their flesh. But I don't believe the dead actually care about those things." I dropped my hands. "Come now, Doctor. How many deaths have you seen? And has any one of them ever returned to complain of how they were laid out?"

"Not one," he admitted. "Still, I would not look for Roderick to leave just yet. Not until he is certain."

"Certain of what?"

"That the dead don't walk," said Denton, closing his lips over his teeth and refusing to say anything more.

The dead don't walk.

The thought beat at my brain like a fragment of song and rang in my ears on an endless loop. I even flexed my jaw in exactly the right way to trigger a bout of tinnitus, but as soon as it passed, the words were there again. *The dead don't walk. The dead don't walk.*

But they *don't*. I had missed my shot at the hare. It was certainly dead by now, bled out somewhere, or a fox had come along and finished the job. Or a weasel, or a hawk. I didn't know the local predators, but presumably they were the same as in Gallacia. A loose dog, a cat from the village. There were no cats in Usher's house.

You get a cat for the rats, I thought, *and there are no rats either. Why are there no rats? Is Roderick so poor that his pantry cannot even tempt a rat?*

It was possible. Though it occurred to me that I had seen no animals around that staring house, except for the horses in the stables and the mad-eyed hares on the heath . . . which brought me back to the hares again.

The dead don't walk.

I rode Hob, despite a light drizzle. The sound of his hoofbeats broke into a rhythm that lent itself all too well to the line. *Clip-clop clip-clop. The-dead don't-walk. The-dead don't-walk. Clip-clop.*

Christ's blood, I was going to break into my third bottle of livrit if this kept up.

Dinner was no relief. Roderick kept absently wringing his fingers together and then catching himself. Denton was even more American than usual. If his accent got any broader, he was going to start singing "The Star-Spangled Banner" and shaking hands with the tablecloth.

The dead don't walk. Except that you're supposed to sit with the dead for three days to make sure they don't. And Roderick had said that he could hear her knocking on the door of the crypt. No, that was ridiculous.

I retired to my chambers and finished off the dregs of

the second bottle of livrit, under Angus's disapproving eye. "Don't scowl so. There's not enough in here to give a hangover to a gnat."

"How long are we going to stay here?" asked Angus.

"I don't know." I licked the syrupy taste off my lips. How long did we stay? Until Roderick agreed to leave, whenever that was? Was I doing any good, or was I just eating food and burning firewood that he could ill afford to spare?

"Three days," I said abruptly, setting the empty bottle down on the table. "Three more days. Then we'll go."

At midnight, I went to the crypt.

It was not a reasonable thing to do. I knew that. For all my vaunted skepticism, the thought had taken hold of me that if no one watched the body, something terrible would happen. Or perhaps it had already happened. The dead don't walk, but what of those with catalepsy? You heard stories of people buried alive, of coffins opened to find that someone had clawed at the lid.

I crept down the slick stone steps, the candle in my hand, trying to make no sound. The crypt door was barred but had no lock. The bar itself was an immense thing, as thick as my wrist. It looked oddly new, with pale edges where the wood had not yet weathered.

I set down the candle and lifted the bar carefully, holding my breath as it scraped against the metal holding it in. Each tiny sound echoed up the steps. *At least I'll be able to hear if anyone comes down behind me,* I thought. *I hope.*

I had no idea what I'd say if anyone did. Plead grief, I suppose. Say that I had to come see her one last time. Remind

Roderick of the superstition that the dead must be watched for three days. I was not that worried about it. People in mourning are allowed to do odd things. This was absolutely a strange thing to be doing. Maddy was dead, I did not doubt it. It was astonishing that she had still been alive when I saw her. She could not have lasted more than a few days. I knew that.

I also knew that I had to see her. Every sense I had honed over years on the battlefield was screaming that something was not as it appeared. I could feel it. *The dead don't walk.*

I picked up the candle and opened the door. A wave of tinnitus rose in my ears and I waited it out, seeing the light flicker on the shrouded form on the slab, the high ringing note pulsing inside my skull.

When it finally faded, I went forward. I stood over the shrouded form of Madeline Usher and set my hand to the cloth . . . and hesitated.

Part of me wanted to abandon this fool quest. Why was I here? Why was I skulking around Roderick's manor like a thief, disturbing his sister's rest? I was an old friend, yes, but I was violating all laws of hospitality and friendship. It was not my place.

But something was still very, very wrong.

I pulled back the shroud and froze.

It was Maddy. She did not seem to have deteriorated at all in two days. The cool air of the crypt might have saved her, though I did not think it was so cold as that. Or perhaps she had simply looked so shocking before she died that mere decay could not worsen it. Her hair clung to the shroud and shed fine white hairs across the stone surface of the slab where I had moved it.

That was not what stunned me.

Her neck had been broken. She had been very carefully arranged, the shroud draped to hide the terrible angle of her throat. And though she had died before they had time to bruise, there were livid finger marks splayed across her throat.

I stood so long that the candle dripped wax past the guard and spilled onto my hand. The sharp burn brought me back to myself, and I tilted it so that none fell on the shroud or the slab or the dead woman's skin.

And then I carefully replaced the shroud and took my candle and crept back up the stairs, moving as silently as a scout on patrol. I was now in enemy territory, and my life and Angus's might very well hang in the balance.

CHAPTER 9

It is very unpleasant to sit down to a meal when you are trying to determine which one of your breakfast companions is a murderer. I drank my tea and met no one's eyes, while my thoughts raced and rattled about my skull.

Denton was the obvious choice. Denton was a doctor. He could not possibly have examined Maddy and *not* noticed the broken neck. But at the same time, as a doctor, he should have had a hundred and one ways to kill someone without resorting to such a crude method of murder.

Still, that was not enough to rule him out. Men panicked sometimes. Perhaps it had been a crime of passion, an unrequited lust for Madeline. I had seen no such indication, but men have hidden such things before. It had to be Denton.

Didn't it?

But just when I had convinced myself thoroughly of Denton's guilt, I would glance at Roderick out of the corner of my eye. If there was ever a man wracked by a guilty conscience, it was Roderick Usher. He startled at every sound, turning his head constantly as if expecting that someone was creeping up on him. One of the servants brought in more tea and he yelped and dropped his fork with a clatter. And there was the way he had reacted when I called him Lady Macbeth. Even if we ignored all that, surely he had helped to lay his sister out on the slab. Surely he would have noticed the broken neck.

No, the most logical answer was that they were both in on it, that whichever one of them had killed her, the other had helped to cover up.

Would Roderick really cover up his sister's murder? And why murder her at all? She was nearly dead already. What possible gain could there be in hastening her death along?

I found that I could believe that Denton would cover for Roderick, but not that Roderick would cover for Denton. I had seen Usher under fire, in the trenches. I knew what sort of man he was. He had plenty of courage but little nerve, and he had loved his sister dearly. I could think of no hold that Denton might have over him that would cause him to cover such a thing. The doctor could hardly be blackmailing Usher, who had nothing worth taking any longer, and Usher's sins, whatever they might be, were not the sort that would cause a man to stand by while his sister's neck was snapped like a . . . like a . . .

Like a hare, I thought, seeing again the staring eye of the witch-hare. I jammed my fork into my eggs and the tines scraped across the plate. Roderick shrieked.

"I'm sorry," he said, covering his face. "I'm sorry. It's this damned problem with my nerves. I hear . . . I think I hear . . ."

"It's all right," I said automatically. I pushed back from the table, no longer hungry. "I think I'll go for a ride."

The weather had not cleared at all. It was still drizzling and the sky was turning an unpleasant shade of greenish gray. I was barely over the causeway when I saw movement in the grass and found a hare staring at me.

I cursed at it and spurred Hob. He didn't deserve that and he bounced a few times to let me know that he knew he didn't deserve that. I didn't look over my shoulder but I could feel the hare behind me, like an enemy sentry watching to see if I strayed into disputed territory. I fancied that as soon as I was out of sight, it would go crawling along to alert the other hares to my presence.

Hares don't do that, of course. Hares aren't like rabbits, who actually post sentries around their warrens and alert each other to danger. Of course, with these accursed things, who knew anymore? Maybe I was right, and there was a disease. Maybe it was making the hares as paranoid as Roderick.

Something clicked inside my head. I was suddenly back in that sheep farmer's hut on the mountain, listening to him rant about sheep diseases. "Th' hydrophobia," he'd allowed. "Aye, they get it. Not th' same as dog, y'hear? Dog gets mean. Sheep gets stupid."

Suppose there was a disease, and it had two forms. One like Madeline's. But Roderick had also declined, hadn't he? Fear. Acute sensitivity to sounds. Could those be symptoms, not of stress but of pathology?

Hob slowed. I looked up, pulled from my thoughts, and saw another hare at the edge of the road, sitting bolt upright. My horse gave it a wide berth and I didn't try to rein him in. For a moment, I was half-afraid the thing might dart out and bite at Hob's legs.

I saw two more of the hares before I made out a far more welcome silhouette, that of Miss Potter sitting on her little stool, umbrella deployed over her head, carefully dabbing at a painting of a mushroom. I was seized with a sudden fear for her, that the hares might be watching her as well. Watching her and preparing to . . . what? Bite? Attack? Spread their disease somehow?

Miss Potter bent over her easel, no doubt in contemplation of boletes or one of the other myriad fungi that infested Usher's land.

Fungi.

A second click inside my head. *Fungi.* I jerked my head up. Not even the blaze of tinnitus that followed the movement could drown the thought. Fungi. Of course. The mold that coated the wallpaper and crept into the library books, the mushrooms that hunched themselves up from the earth, the affliction of Angus's fish?

What had Miss Potter said, upon our first meeting? *I do not know what you know of fungi, but this place is extraordinary . . . so many unusual forms.*

Could it be a fungus, not a disease? Worse, one unique to this region? Was that why Denton could not identify it?

"You said there are fungi that infect living beings," I said, sliding off Hob's back. "You mentioned fish. What about humans?"

"Of course," she said, as if we had been in midconversation and I had not just galloped up to her on horseback as if the Devil himself were on my tail. Hob, always pleased to have an audience, pretended that our great sliding halt had been his idea and pranced to show Miss Potter that she should be impressed. "Ringworm is a fungus. Thrush, which you find on infants, is caused by a yeast that is found on many species. There are others, though some are rare."

"Are any deadly?" I led Hob closer. He rolled his eyes, clearly thinking that it was walk and run and stop and walk and his rider needed to make up kan damn mind.

Miss Potter tapped her finger against her lips. "Yes, though I don't know that they are identified as such as often as they should be. People came back from India with little bumps that covered their face and neck, and that is believed to be a fungus. Men have died of it. And there are molds that form in houses that were strongly believed to contribute to miasma. Now, of course, we have germs, so miasma is no longer in vogue, but I cannot say that the mold could not have weakened a person's lungs so that germs might take hold." She shrugged eloquently. "In short, yes, I believe there are likely fungi that affect humans that are deadly. Certainly they kill fish. And there are the ones that hunt worms, which is not the same as infection, but—"

"Wait, what?" I held up a hand. "Did you say a fungus that hunts *worms*?"

"Oh yes. It caused quite a stir in the proceedings of the Society last year. A German named Zopf discovered a fungus that actively seeks out nematodes."

It was a sign of how disordered my nerves had become that I did not derive nearly enough enjoyment from hearing Miss Potter pronounce the word "nematode" with an accent so British that it very nearly had its own stiff upper lip. I could only imagine packs of mushrooms leaping across the moors in pursuit of prey. It should have been funny. I told myself firmly that it was funny. "Hunt how?"

"Adhesive properties," said Miss Potter. "They secrete a sticky net of hyphae, and once the worm is ensnared, the net cells germinate on the worm and extend a network through it, devouring it."

"Does that kill it?"

"Eventually, yes." Her eyes flicked away. I gathered that it was not a pleasant experience for the worm.

I licked my lips. "Hyphae?"

"Multicellular filaments. What differentiates a mold from a yeast, in essence."

An idea was forming in the back of my mind. I didn't like it one bit. "What do they look like, these hyphae?"

"They can take a number of different forms," said Miss Potter. "But the most common one is white filaments."

"Filaments." I thought of Angus's description of the fish. "Like slimy felt?"

"Felt, certainly, if it's a thick enough mat." She smiled tranquilly up at me. "But in small amounts, it would look like fine white hairs."

"Lieutenant Easton, where *are* we going?"

"A crypt," I said. "It's . . . it's very hard to explain. I just need you to look at something under a magnifying glass."

"Is it a fungus?"

"It's a dead woman's hair."

Miss Potter stopped in the middle of the hallway. I had hustled her into the manor, hopefully without alerting anyone, and was trying to get her down to the crypt. It would have been easier if she hadn't kept stopping and demanding explanations.

"I must assume you refer to Miss Usher? Lieutenant, I have come to think of you as a sensible person, but there is something quite unsavory about all this."

Unsavory seemed like such a dire understatement that I gave a bark of laughter. "I know. It's utterly appalling. But, Miss Potter, I swear to you on my honor as a soldier—"

"I have," she said, in blighting tones, "known far too many soldiers."

I could not argue that. Frankly, I'd only said it because I thought it was the sort of thing that might appeal to an Englishwoman, pip-pip, cheerio, God save the Queen, and so forth. I placed my hand against the peeling wallpaper and took a deep breath.

"Miss Potter," I said, "I swear to you on the graves of soldiers that I have buried with my own hands, I mean no harm to you or anyone in this house. But if I try to explain it, you will think me completely mad. It is easier to show you. And if you tell me that I am mistaken, then I will escort you back to town and make a clean breast of everything to the master of this house."

Eugenia Potter looked at me with her small, bright eyes, then gave a single sharp nod. "Very well. 'Lay on, Macduff!'"

My heart was in my throat that we would meet Denton or Usher or one of the servants on the way to the crypt, but that vast house worked in my favor for once. We saw no one. I led her through increasingly dim corridors, only to realize that I had no lamp or candle.

I swore softly in Gallacian. Miss Potter cocked a jaundiced eye at me. "I do not know what that word means, Lieutenant, but I have my suspicions."

"Sorry, Miss Potter."

"Mm. If you will hold my umbrella, I will provide a light." She reached into her enormous bag and withdrew a small shuttered lantern. It was my turn to stare.

"Miss Potter! Is that a housebreaker's lantern?"

"It is none of my affair what others may use such a design for," she said primly. "The shutters are most useful for providing specific directional lighting when I have been working on a painting long enough that the sun has changed position." She lit the candle inside the lantern and adjusted the shutters, then handed it to me.

"Madam," I said fervently, "you are a wonder."

"Hmmph!"

We navigated the stairs to the crypt with the aid of the lantern. I pulled the bar from the door and pushed it open. The light from the shuttered lantern fell upon the empty slab, the shroud lying forlornly on the floor, and nothing more.

Madeline was gone.

CHAPTER 10

"Lieutenant. *Lieutenant.*"

My ears were ringing so loudly that I could not hear the words, only see Miss Potter's lips moving. I was on my knees. The damp chill of the crypt was sinking into my bones. My shoulder throbbed.

Madeline was gone. Her body was gone. Someone must have moved it. Yes, of course. Usher, perhaps, to conceal his crime. She had been dead for three days, so it was a bit late for that, but it was the only explanation. It was foolishness to think that she might have moved on her own, sat up on the slab, pushed the shroud aside like a blanket. *The dead don't walk.*

"Lieutenant."

I heard that word faintly. It had the force of command to it and I straightened involuntarily. "Yes," I said, probably too loudly. "I apologize. There should be a body here. It was a shock."

Miss Potter helped me to my feet. "Lieutenant, I fear that

after the loss of your friend, your nerves may be somewhat overset."

This was a polite English way of saying that she thought I was a squalling lunatic, and I couldn't argue the point. At least the shroud was still here. I picked it up and spread it across the slab, looking for the white hairs that I had seen.

The relief when I found one was intense. At least this much was real. I pointed to a patch and said, "These. Are these hyphae?"

She gave me a narrow-eyed look, perhaps for dragging her mycology into my madness, but she took out her magnifying glass and set the lantern on the slab to look. I waited with my heart in my throat, looking toward the open door. A tiny voice whispered that it would swing shut and we would hear the bar fall into place and we would be trapped down here. I took a few cautious steps toward the door, wondering if I could rush to it in time if I heard the hinges creak.

"Hmm," said Miss Potter.

"What is it?"

She made an impatient gesture. "Give me time."

"Sorry." I went back to my maudlin imaginings. Would it be Roderick Usher, determined to hide his crime? Or something worse? Would it be a figure in white, animated by some terrible force? The force that had moved a hare missing half its head to stand up and stare?

The dead don't walk. The dead don't *walk.* If they did, then . . . then . . . I don't know what. Something dreadful. I had killed so many people and seen so many die, and what if none of them were peaceful in the ground? What if they were roaming around? What if I would have to face them and explain?

"Definitely hyphae," said Miss Potter, setting down her

magnifying glass. "I would require a stronger glass to state for certain whether it is septate or nonseptate, and I cannot swear that these are not the pseudohyphae found in yeasts. Nevertheless, they are not human hairs, nor fabric threads."

"What if I told you those were growing out of human skin?"

Miss Potter made a well-bred motion of her chin that, in another person, would have been a vast shrug. "Saprophytic fungi—ah, that is to say, those that feed upon decaying organic matter—are exceedingly common. Unsightly, perhaps, but they pose no threat to living creatures."

"Madeline was alive at the time," I said, holding her gaze, "and there were so many of them on her skin that I thought her body hair had turned white."

The English, in my experience, make an enormous deal about the most minor inconveniences, but if you confront them with something world-shattering, they do not blink. Miss Potter did blink, but only once, and then she looked down at her magnifying glass and said, "I see."

"Could that be what sickened her?" I asked.

"If the fungus was so widespread that it was sending filaments through her skin . . . yes. Certainly." The stiffness of her upper lip was magnificent to behold. "But what has become of her body?"

The dead don't walk. Most likely Roderick moved the body, to further conceal his crime. And Denton must know that something is wrong with Roderick, and helped him cover it up, but he doesn't know the cause. If he knows what it is, perhaps he can treat it. "I don't know. But I must tell Denton."

"Indeed," she said. "You must tell everyone. If this is a fungus that can spread on a living host, it must be stopped immediately." She reached into her bag and took out a small silver flask, which she dumped over her hands. I could smell the sting of alcohol from where I stood. "Give me your hands, Lieutenant. You touched the shroud."

"I touched Madeline," I said grimly. "Several times. The hyphae tore away in my hands."

Her eyes lifted to mine. "Then we shall hope that this is effective even after the fact."

I listened to the dripping of spirits on the crypt floor as she sloshed whiskey over my fingers, then rubbed my hands together. Were the hares also infected? How could I tell? What were a few more white threads in a hare's pelt?

The fish. *Like slimy felt,* Angus had said. Did the fungus originate in the tarn after all? Had it jumped from fish to hare, perhaps when the hares came down to drink?

Had Angus touched it himself?

And where the hell was Madeline's body?

"Denton," I cried, bursting into the study. "Madeline's gone!"

He stared at me for a long moment, then his face softened and he reached out and touched my arm. "I know," he said gently. "I know. But she's not suffering any longer, and—"

"No, you blithering idiot," I growled, shaking his hand off. Damnable English language—more words than anybody can be expected to keep track of, and then they use the same one for about three different things. "I *know* she's dead! I'm telling you, her body's gone!"

Denton blinked at me. "What?"

"She's not in the crypt. The slab is empty. We cannot *habeas* the *corpus*. Is any of this getting through?" (I was, perhaps, rather less reverent than the situation warranted, but it is a flaw of mine that I become sarcastic when I am frustrated.)

"Are you serious?"

Miss Potter coughed politely behind me. "I can assure you, young man, that the lieutenant is quite correct."

"Miss Potter? What are—?" Denton obviously started to question her presence, then just as obviously abandoned it for more important things. "No. Later. This is dreadful."

"Do you think Roderick moved her?" I asked.

I was expecting him to look away from guilt, but he met my eyes squarely. "Perhaps."

"You know there's something wrong with him," I said softly. "You know what he did—"

Denton cut my words off with a slicing motion of his hand. "This is not the time."

"Well, then let us find Roderick and—"

"He's asleep," said Denton.

"Then we'll wake him and—"

"I gave him a sleeping pill," said Denton. "He won't wake up for hours. No, don't glare so, Lieutenant. He says he can't sleep at all, that he hears his sister walking in the crypt. I don't think he's gotten an hour straight of sleep since she died."

"That's what I'm trying to tell you. This bizarre malady of his—it's the same thing Madeline had."

Denton blinked at me. "What?"

"It's not a disease! It's a fungus! I—oh, for pity's sake, Miss Potter, you tell him."

Miss Potter drew Denton aside and explained, in what I assume was English, about saprophytic fungi and the hyphae. I stared at the wall and wondered if Roderick had moved Maddy's body out of guilt or some notion that he would stop hearing her walk if she was no longer in the crypt. Christ's blood! Now that we knew what it was, could we treat it somehow?

"Possible," Denton was saying. "It's possible. I would not have thought it, but no doctor worth his salt will ever say that he's seen everything there is to see. But I don't see how we can prove it. The shroud may have been moldy, after all."

"An autopsy on Maddy's body would show it," I said shortly.

"A body that you tell me we don't have. And I am certainly not going to slice open Roderick's skin looking for these hyphae!"

I gritted my teeth. "Then it'll have to be a hare. And this time I won't miss."

It was Angus who provided the hare. I had swallowed my pride and gone to him to ask for his help. "Not for eating, I won't!" he said, but when I explained that it was going to be dissected, he put his head to one side and said, "How fresh do you be needin' it?"

"Eh?"

"There's one not a hundred feet from t'end of the causeway. Fell in the lake, by the look of it. Saw it on my way back from the village this morning."

We tromped out to find it. Sure enough, there one was, lying half-in, half-out of the water, facedown. It looked as if it had simply wandered up to the tarn and fallen asleep.

I was wearing my riding gloves, but I went back for a long stick from the woodpile, and fished it out without touching the water. Angus raised his eyebrows at me, but didn't comment.

There were four of us assembled around the breakfast table this time, although what was laid out was substantially less appetizing. The light was the best in the house, and that was all that we could hope for. We had brought in lamps and candles from our rooms and crowded them along the table until the table was drowning in light. Denton had fetched his doctor's bag and opened it, a black leather mouth gleaming with scalpel teeth.

"Miss Potter," said Angus, touching his cap. "'Tis a pleasure to see you again."

Miss Potter actually went a little pink. "Mr. Angus. I didn't think I'd see you so soon."

"You two met, then?" Come to think of it, Angus hadn't been complaining about the lack of occupation lately, but I had been too distracted to pay attention.

"Oh yes. Mr. Angus was kind enough to hold my umbrella at just the right angle the other day while I painted a particularly fine *Amanita phalloides.*"

I was trying to come up with a joke about *phalloides* that would not end with Miss Potter hitting me with her umbrella when Denton cleared his throat and called us back to reality. "I am making the first incision," he said.

"Wait!" Miss Potter looked around the room, found a stack of linen napkins, and hastily handed them around. "Cover your mouth and nose. If there are spores, and this is indeed a dangerous fungus, we do not wish to inhale them."

I knotted the napkin around my head. Denton muttered something about feeling like he was about to rob a stagecoach, then took up the scalpel again. We watched in silence as the blade parted fur and skin, then cut deeper.

It was hard to tell what might be hyphae. The ligaments that connect skin to flesh are also pale and very fine. But once he opened up the chest with shears, it became clear that *something* had been very wrong with the hare.

"Slimy felt," said Angus. "Like the blood—Beggin' your pardon, ma'am. Like the blasted fish."

Denton touched the matted surface gingerly with the tip of the scalpel. It did indeed look as if something was adhering to the surface of the organs, something slimy and fibrous, though it was a dark reddish color instead of the brilliant white of the hyphae on Madeline's arms. The red stuff looked almost like the seaweed you see dried along the rocks on the coast, forming a sticky membrane over everything.

"The animal is female," said Denton dispassionately. *And if it were human, would it be diagnosed with hysterical catalepsy?* I thought.

Miss Potter took out her magnifying glass and bent over the animal. If being six inches from the animal's viscera troubled her, she gave no sign. "Fungal," she confirmed.

"Would that be enough to kill it?" I asked.

"There is no way of telling," she said, folding the magnifying glass back into its case. "We know nothing about this fungus, about its malignancy, about how long it would take to grow to this extent. Some molds can spread incredibly quickly, and this hare has presumably been dead for some time."

"Looked like it drowned," volunteered Angus.

"If it drowned, presumably its lungs are full of water," Denton said, drawing the scalpel almost absently across the left lung.

The tissue retracted and the contents bulged out in a sticky white mass. It looked like cotton wool, erupting from the chest cavity as if it had been packed in too tightly to contain. Denton jerked back with a curse.

"I will go out on a limb," I said, "and say that's not normal for drowning."

"Good God," said Denton. He opened up the other lung and the white woolen mat of fungus bulged out there, too. He grabbed a fork off the table and began digging around. I felt my gorge rise. I've field dressed any number of animals and I don't mind guts, but this was something else again.

Denton shook his head slowly, setting down the fork. "The lungs are packed with it. That's not possible. Lungs aren't hollow, they're like a honeycomb, but this stuff got in and . . . it looks like it just ate the interior away somehow."

"A warm moist growth medium," said Miss Potter, "is very conducive to the growth of many, many fungi."

"Yes, but it can't possibly have lived through—"

The animal moved.

There were three veterans at that table, battle-scarred soldiers who had served their countries honorably in more than one war . . . and all three of us screamed like small children and recoiled in horror.

The hare kicked twice, not seeming to care that its guts were open to the air, and managed to roll itself over. Angus flung himself in front of Miss Potter. I flung myself backward in my chair, knocking it over and taking me with it. This proved to be providential, because Denton flung his scalpel aside and would have speared me handily with it if I hadn't been on my back on the floor.

By the time I was upright, the hare was crawling along the table, leaving a broad pink smear across the tablecloth. Denton was in the corner, quivering, and Angus looked dazed.

Miss Potter flipped her umbrella around and pinned the hare in place with the tip. "Gentlemen," she said, "I will hold it in place if one of you would like to kill it. Again."

Moving almost mechanically, I reached into Denton's bag and pulled out a heavy blade that looked like kin to a meat cleaver. The hare twitched and paddled its feet against the tablecloth. The thin taste of bile coated my tongue.

One solid chop with the cleaver severed the hare's spine, and it fell limp. I did not stop until the body had been fully detached from the head, and even then I might have kept going, but Angus took the cleaver away from me.

"It's done," he said.

"It isn't," said Miss Potter. "The head is still moving."

I looked at the head pinned under the umbrella and saw the mouth opening and closing, the chisel teeth catching in the tablecloth, and then my gorge rose and I turned and ran to the privy.

When I was empty of even the memory of food, I dragged myself back to the drawing room. They had thrown the tablecloth over the twitching hare and wrapped it into a featureless ball. Denton was as white as the linen napkin over his face as he stood repacking his bag. "The fungus grew in greatest concentration at the top of the spinal column," he said, in a distant, precise voice. "It had completely wrapped the vertebrae there and intruded into the skull."

"But severing the spine killed the body," I said. The image of Madeline's corpse, her head bent, intruded behind my eyes.

"*No.*" He slammed the bag shut. "That hare has been dead

for days. Whatever that thing is, it was moving it around like a puppet. All we did was cut the main strings."

"Nor will they stay cut," said Miss Potter. She sounded the calmest of the four of us. "The growth rate of some fungi, as I said, is extraordinary. I suspect that if we left this specimen alone long enough, it would regrow the connections and begin to move again."

"Christ's blood." I put my head in my hands. The dead don't walk. Except, sometimes, when they do. "Then Madeline . . ."

"*Don't.*" Denton nearly shouted the word. After a moment, he said, "Let's get rid of this thing. I can't . . . I can't think about the other thing. Not yet."

"Throw it in the lake, then?" I said.

"I do not recommend that, Lieutenant. If it comes in contact with the water supply, it could infect anyone who drinks the water."

Angus's mustache sagged. So did the rest of him. "Miss Potter," he said quietly, "it's in the lake already. It's in the fish. All our drinking water comes from the lake. All of us—the three of us—have been drinking it and bathing in it for days."

"Weeks for me," said Denton.

Miss Potter, to her credit, did not recoil in horror from us. She nodded once, slowly, and said, "Then I am afraid, gentlemen, that there is a chance that all of you have contracted it already."

Denton nodded to himself. I looked down at my arms, picturing the skin under the fabric with its fine dark hairs. If I shoved the sleeves back, would there be long white strands emerging from the surface?

"We'll burn it," I said, grabbing the bundle of cloth. I fancied I could feel a quiver of motion inside. "Angus, bring lamp oil."

The stable yard was empty, the horses tucked away in their stalls. (Oh God, was the foul stuff inside Hob, too? Had I killed him by bringing him here?) We passed through it to the ragged garden, to the burn pile. It was pitifully small. Every scrap that could be used to heat the house had already been scavenged.

I dropped the tablecloth and its contents onto the darkened paving stones and Angus emptied one of the lamps over the cloth, then knelt and lit it. We stood shoulder to shoulder around it in a semicircle, close enough to feel the heat of the flame, unwilling to leave until the beast had been reduced to ash. Occasionally Angus would stir it with a stick, and we used Roderick's lamp oil recklessly to finish the job.

It was thus some time before we had finished, and the evening was drawing in. When we turned back to the house, Miss Potter's startled cry froze us all.

"What is that light?"

Sickly greenish radiance haloed the near end of the house. It was faint enough that perhaps we would not have seen it if the sky had been brighter, but against the darkness, it stood out in sharp relief.

"A fire?" said Denton, although not as if he believed it. "A . . . chemical fire?"

We had only to go a little way before the edge of the tarn came into view, and that answered the question while raising many new ones.

The lake was glowing.

It was the same thing I had seen days before, the pulsing lights that seemed to chase one another along the edges of unseen shapes, but far brighter than last time. The glow picked up the faint mist that had settled across the lake and turned it into a cloud of sickly light. The waters themselves seemed to pulse like a heartbeat, but far more rapidly than any human heart. I wondered how it compared to a hare's heartbeat, and then I looked around.

Not too far away, its eyes lit with reflected green fire, a hare stood and watched.

"Angus—"

"I see it."

The four of us went very slowly around the edge of the tarn. The lights grew brighter. The hare did not follow and it was too dark to make out any others. My skin crawled with awareness.

At last we stood before the causeway that led into the house. "Well," said Miss Eugenia Potter, gazing into the flickering water, "I can tell you that has *not* been recorded in the annals of mycology."

"How do we destroy a fungus?" I asked Miss Potter. "Quick! How does something like this die?"

She tore her eyes away from the lake and stared at me blankly. "Antifungals?" she said finally. "There are woods with antifungal properties . . . some powders . . . hydrogen peroxide, perhaps . . . ?"

"You don't know?"

"I draw mushrooms, Lieutenant! I am usually trying to keep them alive!"

I put my head in my hands.

"We used to treat foot fungus with alcohol, in the army," said Denton. "Have them soak their feet in it."

"Certainly that could work, but how much alcohol do you have available?" asked Miss Potter. "Can you drown the full tarn?"

"I've got a bottle of livrit," I said. "And presumably there's still a wine cellar, although it may be somewhat picked over."

Miss Potter's expression indicated that the wine cellar was not going to work.

"Never mind," I said, watching the pulsing lights. "Never mind, never mind. We'll deal with it. I'll deal with it. Angus . . ." I turned. "Angus, I want you to get Miss Potter away from here. Take Hob. If you can get a wagon, leave him at the stable, and if any of us live . . . Oh, Christ's blood. Both our horses might be infected."

"I'll sort it," said Angus. I had no doubts. He'd made his entire career sorting logistics far more complicated than a couple of horses.

"Lieutenant!" Miss Potter began, drawing herself up to her full height, which was taller than mine, and glared down at me. "I assure you, I am not some shrinking violet who requires an escort to safety, lest I faint!"

"Miss Potter," I said, "I would never dream of suggesting it. But you are the only person who has the faintest idea what, scientifically, we may be dealing with here, and who has any hope of explaining it to the authorities in a way that does not sound completely mad. And if there is an infection, or infestation, or . . . whatever you would call this . . . the authorities must be warned. Angus will go with you to make certain that you are taken seriously, because . . . well . . ." I leaned in and said, in an undertone, "You know what men are like when women try to tell them anything."

Miss Potter's expression thawed. She sighed heavily and picked up her umbrella. "You are not wrong there, Lieutenant. Very well." She gave the glowing tarn one last, grim look.

They vanished into the stable and emerged moments later. Miss Potter rode Hob, who seemed somewhat astonished but who was on his very best manners. "That's an English gentlewoman you're carrying," I admonished him. "Probably fifteenth in line to the throne. You be polite."

"More like a hundred and fifteenth," said Miss Potter, "a fact which gives me great comfort." She patted Hob's neck. "Please take *extremely* good notes on what happens with the lake, Lieutenant. I do so hate to miss this."

"I shall make observations that will cause the Royal Mycology Society to tremble in their boots," I promised. "Angus, watch for hares."

"Aye. And watch your own skin, youngster. I'm too old to break in another officer."

They hurried away down the road, as fast as they could safely move in the dark. I watched them go, then turned to Denton.

"Now what?" he said, staring into the lake. The light show was beginning to wane, though flickers of light still went racing through the dark water at intervals.

"All right," I said grimly. "They're gone. Now we talk."

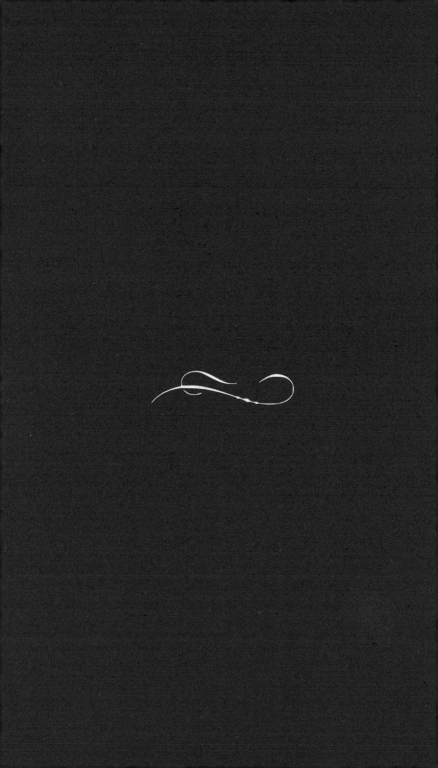

CHAPTER 11

"I know her neck's been broken," I said. "Roderick, I assume?"

Denton inhaled sharply. "How did you know?" he asked.

"I went down to the crypt and looked."

"Ah." He grimaced. "It wasn't murder, if that's what you mean. Well, it was, but it's not—that is—" He rubbed his face. "I need a drink."

"I'll pour. And tell me everything."

I would have burned my last bottle of livrit in such a just cause, but fortunately Denton had his own brandy. His rooms did not look much different than mine, although he had no man to help him.

"Roderick called me in a month ago," he said, collapsing into a chair. It sent up a puff of dust and probably mold spores, but really, what was one more set at this point?

"For the catalepsy."

"Not exactly." He took a swig of brandy. "It was the madness that concerned him."

"What madness was that?"

Denton groaned, got up, and fished through his belongings until he came up with a battered envelope. "Here. No sense in playing twenty questions when you can just read it."

I recognized Roderick's spidery handwriting as I unfolded the letter. He wasted no time on salutations.

Denton—

I need your help. There's something desperately wrong with Madeline, more than just the catalepsy that has afflicted her for some years. Since her near-drowning, she has fallen under the spell of a strange madness, one that leaves her speaking in ways entirely unlike herself. She will be entirely herself one morning, and then by afternoon, I will find her speaking to the servants as if she is a small child. She points at things and asks for their names and seems astonished. Her voice is very strange. When I confront her, she will revert immediately to her old self, but she acts very strange and sly, saying that it was merely a moment of muddle-headedness.

What she is doing is frightening the servants. Worst of all, I have heard someone speak this way before, but it was Alice, her maid, who spoke in such fashion. I would overhear them sometimes in Madeline's room. At the time, I thought Alice was doing impressions to make her laugh.

You will think me quite deluded, Denton, but when I hear this voice she speaks in, I begin to think of stories of demonic possession, not of illness. It is very terrible to witness.

I know that you are a man of reason, and I strive to

be, though this dreadful estate has acted badly on my nerves. Please, I beg of you, if there is any kindness in your heart left for either of us, come and help me.

The signature was Roderick's. I read the letter twice, remembering the strange way that Madeline had spoken that night I found her sleepwalking, the way that she had counted. *Not Maddy,* she'd said.

If she wasn't Maddy, who was she?

"You don't believe in possession, of course," I said, looking up.

"'There are more things in heaven and earth, Horatio' . . . but no, I don't believe in that particular one." He paused, then said, very quietly, "*Didn't* believe in that particular one."

"And now?"

Denton shook his head. "I don't know what I believe anymore. When I spoke to Madeline, she was exactly as she had always been. Until she wasn't."

"Explain."

"I can't. Not rationally. She seemed to undergo some kind of mental shift, and then her speech changed. Not like anything I've seen before." He stared at the ceiling. "Slurred speech with aphasia, which is about as useful a diagnosis as catalepsy. Most of us get that when we're drunk, for God's sake. I'm a cut-rate surgeon, Easton, I chop off *limbs*. I'm not an alienist." He scowled. "I told you that she almost drowned, yes?" I nodded and he continued. "Roderick thought—and I begin to agree—that there was nothing *almost* about it. He told me that she had been in the water for hours when he found her."

I stared at him, willing the words to make sense, and couldn't. "What?"

"I thought he'd lost it," said Denton bluntly. "Time slows when you panic, of course. He pulled her out and thought that it was much too late. So he took her down to the crypt and sobbed over her for half the night."

I swallowed. "And?"

"And she woke up. And began speaking to him in that voice he found so upsetting."

"How is that possible? Could she really have drowned?" I didn't know why I was asking, when I had seen the hare twitching, but hares are not the same as humans, are they?

Denton shook his head. "Drowning is strange," he admitted. "People come back sometimes, long after you'd think they were gone, particularly when they've been in cold water. That's what I told Roderick, anyway, when he insisted she had been in the water more than a few minutes." He sank back into the chair. "And I went on believing that Madeline was just groggy from waking up after a fright, and Roderick had panicked and believed she was in the water far longer than she was."

"And it was after this that she began to manifest this . . . this otherness."

Denton nodded again. "I thought the drowning had little to do with it. It seemed more likely that it was a result of the suicide of her maid. They were close. Perhaps she was trying to keep a game they had played alive somehow."

"And now?"

He snorted. "Now it's obvious, isn't it? It's this fungus. It's causing this altered state somehow. First in the maid, then in Madeline. Perhaps it's a hallucinogenic effect of some sort, or perhaps simple poisoning."

"Why kill her?" It was a measure of how far I had come

that I could ask the question without any particular condemnation.

"Roderick says he didn't mean to kill her, but the thing that had taken over her body."

"So the fungus got into her from the lake and now it's affected her, made her act this way. . . ."

"So it would seem." Denton's face was bleak. After a moment he said, tonelessly, "After he killed her, I didn't know what to do. I didn't know what was going on, but Roderick said it was evil and it was devouring Maddy, and . . . God have mercy on me, I can't say he was wrong."

I thought of Maddy's smile that night, the flat-eyed rictus, and the way that I had recoiled from it. *Evil* might not be the right word, but I could see how Roderick had come to it. "So you covered for him."

"Yes. I know it was wrong, but . . ." He lifted his hands and let them drop. "He's dying, too. I can't imagine him lasting much longer in this state."

"All right," I said. "All right." I tried to formulate the words that had to be spoken and then drained my brandy instead. I would have liked to get extremely drunk. I would have liked to get on a horse and ride away as fast as its hooves could carry me, but Hob was gone and Angus with him. Both Denton and I knew the truth, but saying the words would make it real, and dear God, how I wanted it not to be real.

I set the tumbler down and took a deep breath. "Madeline's like the hare now," I continued grimly. "That's why she's not on the slab. This thing is moving her around."

I don't know how long we sat there after that, drinking our courage. Too long, probably. But sooner or later you have to act or resign yourself to not acting at all.

"We have to find her body," I said, rising from my chair.

"She must still be in the crypt," said Denton. "Surely it can't move her very far."

I stared at him, then realized that he had not seen the hares and their terrible ratcheting crawl, only the one on the table who had managed a few feet before being stopped. "I think, perhaps, it can do a bit more than that," I said.

Denton picked up the bottle and drained it dry. "We can't let Roderick see her like this," he said. "We'll have to burn the body."

I nodded and picked up a lamp. So did Denton. I still had my pistol, but what good would shooting Maddy's corpse do? It hadn't stopped the hare.

The crypt steps were cold and dark and both Denton and I were jumpy. Every movement of the lamps made the shadows flicker and whenever one loomed too large, we both recoiled.

"You'd think we were a pair of children, not soldiers," I muttered. Denton mumbled something under his breath that I didn't quite catch.

A dozen steps from the bottom, I stopped. Denton nearly ran into my back. I lifted the lamp high, revealing the crypt door.

The *unbarred* crypt door.

The door that was now ajar.

"Why did you stop?" whispered Denton.

"The door's open."

"Did you close it before?"

"I thought I had." I hadn't barred it, though. Why bar a door to an empty crypt? "Could Roderick have gone in?"

"Roderick shouldn't even be able to get up to piss in the pot," said Denton. He paused, then added grudgingly, "Of course, I've been nothing but wrong since the beginning, so my medical opinion isn't worth a plug nickel."

I wondered what the hell a plug nickel was, but it didn't seem like the time to ask. I went down the last few steps and pushed the door aside.

The slab was still empty. "Maddy?" I called. The echoes rushed through the room like birds, and I could hear my voice ringing faintly down the corridor on the far side of the crypt, into the catacombs where generations of Ushers lay moldering.

No answer. I listened for any sound at all: a rustle of winding cloths, the sound of a body dragging itself along, one limb at a time.

Nothing.

"She isn't here," I said.

"She's got to be," said Denton. "You can't tell me she managed all those stairs."

"Why not?" A suspicion had been forming in the back of my brain for hours now and I had been fighting it down. If I didn't put it into words, I could pretend I wasn't thinking it at all.

"Because she's dead! And it's a fungus, not a . . . not a . . ." He groped for words. "It's a glorified mushroom! Maybe it can make a body flail around, but that's all! She must have just rolled off the slab. . . ."

I lifted the lamp, splashing light in the corners of the room. "Look around, Denton. Do you see her?"

He strode forward, rounding the slab, clearly expecting to find the body there. I would have been offended that he thought Miss Potter and I could have missed an entire corpse, but I had a feeling that he had thoughts of his own that he was trying to avoid.

Not finding a body, he went all the way around the slab again, then took a few steps toward the corridor deeper into the catacombs. Then he stopped, clearly thinking better of it. "Are you certain you closed the door?" he asked.

"Yes. The bar I might have forgotten, but we would have closed the door." I raised my hand. "I know, I know doors are too complicated for a fungus to figure out. But here we are."

"It must have been Roderick. Or one of the servants. Your man Angus, if you told him . . ."

"It was *not* Angus."

"A servant, then."

I just looked at him. He growled and stalked back to the corridor, lamp in hand. I went after him, not wanting him to vanish into the depths of the catacombs alone. *What if Madeline is in there? Waiting?*

I looked down and stopped short with a hiss.

"What?" Denton turned, the flame reflecting an orange pinprick in his eyes.

"Look at the floor. Look at the *dust.*"

It had been years since the dust of the corridor was disturbed. Perhaps decades. I could not remember how long it had been since Roderick's father died. It lay in a thick carpet across the floor.

Two lines of footprints stood out in stark relief. Someone with small feet had shuffled through here, not long ago. Their feet had dragged along the floor, leaving smeared lines, but every few feet, the imprint of bare toes was unmistakable. Then they had come back the other way.

Denton swallowed convulsively. "Someone came this way."

"Someone. Yes. And then came back." I took a step back, toward the main crypt. Gratitude flashed across his face and then the two of us rushed back the way we had come. (We did not run. If we ran then we would have to admit there was something to run from. If we ran, then the small child that lives in every soldier's heart knew that the monsters could get us. So we did not run, but it was a near thing.)

The door was still open. The floor here was too overwritten with too many footprints to hold any clues as to who had gone where. I went to the crypt door, trying to think. Heavy wood, with ornate iron scrollwork, as Gothic as the rest of the damned manor. Madeline had been a little shorter than I was. If she had reached out to the door . . .

"Denton."

"What?"

I pointed silently. Next to the iron ring, just where someone's arm would fall if they leaned their weight against the door, was a metal cross. Caught along the edge were a dozen fine white hairs.

I expected Denton to argue, to tell me that it must have been the shroud brushing against the door. But he stared at the white hairs for a long, long moment, and then he breathed out all at once and squared his shoulders. "I see."

"She walked into the catacombs by herself. And walked out again later." And had done so on two feet, and operated the door.

He nodded once, not taking his eyes off the door.

"Denton," I said, "I think we must face the possibility that Madeline is . . ." I struggled for a word, and finally settled on ". . . conscious."

"It's impossible," he said, almost casually. "But that hasn't stopped anything so far, has it?"

"Why is it impossible?"

"Because she's dead. And mushrooms aren't conscious."

"Suppose she isn't dead. No, listen to me. You said people drown sometimes and they come back long after they should have been dead, yes?"

"Hours after, Lieutenant. Not days."

"Suppose the fungus kept her alive. It lives in water, yes? So it can survive drowning. What if it did something so that its host survived, too?"

Denton finally did look at me, opening his mouth, then closed it again. I could practically see him thinking it through. "Brains die from lack of oxygen," he said slowly. "If this fungus could somehow provide oxygen . . . absorb it and pass it to the brain . . . yes, all right. It's a damfool notion and I shouldn't believe it for a second, but if it's already in the brain stem, why not?"

"Madeline wakes up, a few days after her neck is broken," I said. "She gets up and walks into the catacombs. Miss Potter and I come down and then leave, and she comes back to the crypt and finds the door unbarred. She opens it and goes out." I gestured up the steps.

"Which means she's somewhere in the house." Denton sounded amused, but I recognized it as the humor that men get when they see the line of cannons pulled into position. *Ha, yes, of course the enemy has cannons, why wouldn't they? Oh, and we're out of bullets, you say? Ha!*

"Yes."

"Where would she go?"

"Where do you think?" I started up the stairs. "Where would you go, if somebody broke *your* neck? She'd go after Roderick."

This time we did run. We pounded up the stairs. Denton led the way to Roderick's chambers. Our bouncing lamps filled the halls with shadowy giants. If we weren't careful, we'd spill the oil and burn the whole damn place down.

The upper hall was already lit, not by candles but by a pale, sickly light through the window at the end of the hall. Christ, it was dawn already. How long had we sat drinking and trying to get our minds around this? How long had we spent in the crypt?

How long had Madeline been alone with her helpless brother?

Roderick's door opened outward into the hall and stood ajar now. Denton and I shared one frantic glance and then both of us tried to jam ourselves through the doorway simultaneously. I was marginally faster and so I was the one who burst into Roderick's room, pistol in one hand and lamp in the other, to find Madeline.

Sitting on Roderick's bed.

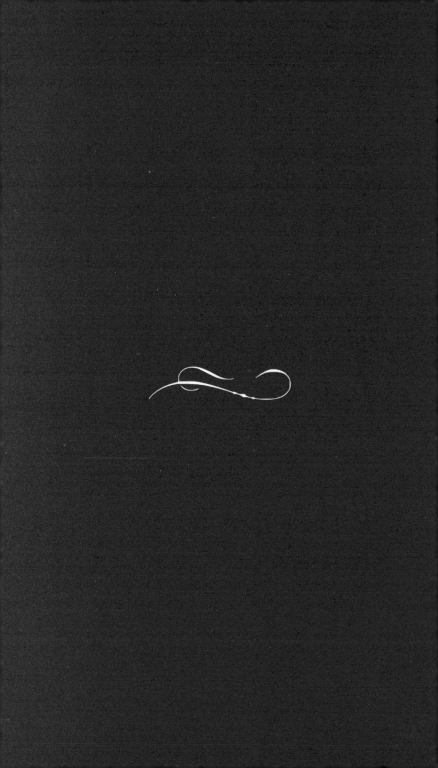

CHAPTER 12

Her head was bent over at a terrible angle, neck horribly askew. She had to turn her whole body to face the door, while her head flopped sideways. She hitched up one shoulder to keep it partly upright and something about that small gesture was so dreadful that it stopped me in my tracks.

"Alex," she said. Her voice was shallow and breathy, as if she could not draw in much air. Were her lungs felted with fungus, like the hare? Was it simply that her neck was broken? Did it even matter?

"Madeline." Roderick was still lying on the bed, on his side. I could not tell if he was breathing. Had she killed him? *And if she has, was it murder or simply justice?*

"Shooting . . . me . . . won't . . . do much . . ." she whispered. Her hair was loose and fell over her eyes, white hair on bone-colored skin. When she lifted her hand to push it away, her fingers were violet-black and a long line ran down the underside of her arms. You see that in dead men sometimes, when the blood has pooled. Whatever the fungus was doing to her, Madeline's heart had stopped beating days ago.

She coughed and her voice gained a little strength. "I suppose . . . I wouldn't enjoy it, though." She smiled ruefully at me, and it was her familiar smile, the one I'd known since we were children.

"Oh God, Maddy," I said. I lowered the gun. Did I really think I could shoot her? "Oh God. What's happened to you?"

"The broken neck was . . . a problem," she said musingly. "The tarn had just been in . . . my brain . . . and my skin. Now va had to grow all the way down . . . past the break. It took . . . days." She shook her head at me, flopping it from side to side. I could see the sharp angle of her windpipe. Nausea clawed at me. "Clever . . . of Roderick. He never understood . . . the tarn."

Denton had come up beside me, his eyes on the bed. "Is Roderick alive, Madeline?"

"I didn't . . . kill him." She coughed again and her head slipped off her shoulder, bouncing in time. I had to look away. When I looked back, she had reached up to her mouth and was tugging. Long white strands came out and she wrapped them around her hand, then let them fall carelessly in her lap. "There," she said, her voice stronger. "There, that's a little better. Va filled my lungs, you see. To save me, but now there's too much." She pushed her head back up onto her shoulder.

"Va?" Who was she referring to like a child?

"The tarn." She smiled up at me. "It's always been the tarn."

Denton took a step forward. "May I examine Roderick?" he asked. It was the right thing to do, of course, but I was desperate to find out what Madeline meant, and why she was referring to the lake as one would a child.

"Yes."

Denton circled the bed as cautiously as if it contained an unexploded shell. Madeline ignored him. I wondered how fast she could move. I caught myself rubbing the trigger guard with my finger and stopped. Terrible habit. Angus would have yelled at me.

"Maddy," I said, hoping to hold her attention. "What do you mean, it's always been the tarn?"

"Va's been reaching out for so long," she said wistfully. "Va could get into the animals. Va learned van senses that way. I can't imagine what that must have been like, the first time. Think of it, if you had no sight and not even the sense that sight existed, how would you get there? Hearing was easier. Va understood vibrations, and that's all hearing is. And va already knew smell." She pointed to her eyes. "But how would you ever think that these two round sacs of jelly did anything? But the tarn figured it out!"

I swallowed. Behind Madeline, Denton gave me a thumbs-up. Roderick was still alive. Thank Christ.

"You're telling me that the tarn is intelligent," I said.

She smiled up at me. "More than you or I are. Think of all va's managed to learn."

"And . . ." Denton was tugging on Roderick's wrist, possibly trying to get him out of bed. "The tarn talks to you? Communicates with you somehow?" Half of me thought that she'd gone mad. The other half pointed out that I was already having a conversation with a dead woman. *Mushrooms don't think. Yes, and the dead don't move either.*

"Speech was the hardest," said Madeline. She plucked another puff of hyphae from her lips. "I had to teach van a kind of sign language first. Va didn't understand speech at all." She giggled again, the papery rasping giggle that set my teeth on edge, made even worse by the impossible angle of her windpipe. "When you think about it, we talk by coughing up air and wiggling our lips through it. How could anyone ever understand that, if you weren't born to it? But va grasped it eventually!"

Breath moving hard, I thought. *Not Maddy. Maddy one and me one . . .*

Oh God, it was *the tarn talking. She taught the fungus to talk.*

There had been clues in front of me, but how could I have possibly guessed the truth? How could I have known that when Maddy was naming the wall and the candle and counting, it was actually a *vocabulary lesson*?

How could I possibly have known that she would treat the fungus like a child?

Denton had gotten Roderick out of bed. The last male Usher looked groggy and leaned against Denton like a drunk, but he was moving. I heard him mumble a question and Denton shushed him.

Madeline started to turn and I stepped forward hastily to distract her. "You taught . . . van . . . the tarn . . . how to talk?"

It worked. She beamed at me. "Once va realized we were using sound to communicate, va almost taught vanself. So smart! My maid and I—va'd take over Alice and then I'd teach van what I could. But then Alice killed herself, that silly creature, and it got harder." A flash of something crossed over her face, sorrow or anger or disappointment, I couldn't tell.

"She killed herself?"

"She didn't understand." Madeline started to stand. One hand snaked out to grab the bedpost, almost as if it were disconnected from the rest of her. "She didn't understand what va was trying to do, and then her fool brother took her body away and burned it, can you imagine? So she couldn't even come back!"

Fire stops it, then, I thought, and a wave of unutterable relief passed over me. If it got into me, as long as Angus burned my body, it would be all right. *The dead may walk, but I will not walk among them.*

"But *you* understand, Easton. You can take over teaching the tarn. Va can't keep my body going much longer, I'm afraid. I'm starting to fray at the edges. Some things break down after a while." She smiled ruefully again and took a step forward.

She moved like the hares and finally I understood.

Maddy's control of her body stopped at the neck. Below the break, the tarn was controlling her body like a puppet.

I stood frozen for far too long, watching her approach. "Madeline," I said carefully, "this thing . . . whatever it is . . . it's what was killing you. Devouring you alive." I would not call the fungus *va.* Never that. It was a horror and it had eaten my friend.

"I know, I know," said Madeline. She dismissed this with a roll of her eyes. "Of course va did. Va doesn't mean to. Va slowed the process as much as va could, but va couldn't help but feed a little. Of course I died eventually."

Denton and I looked at each other over her head. I hope my face was expressionless. His was not.

"You know that you are dead," I said.

Madeline's smile was beatific. "Easton," she said, as kindly as if I were a child, "I've been dead for at least a month."

The tarn stretched out one of her hands and I recoiled. There were puffs of hyphae like cotton wool growing from under her fingernails, shockingly white against the bruise-black skin. Her touch had alarmed me days ago. Knowing what I knew now . . . *Christ's blood. At least fire works. If I can get the lamp oil on her . . . no, this can't be nearly enough. It took so much to burn the hare.* Oh God, why are bodies so *wet*?

Denton was half leading, half carrying Roderick back around the bed. I eased myself a little to one side, trying to place myself between Madeline and the other two. "How is that possible? You were breathing. You had a heartbeat."

"The tarn kept my heart beating as long as va could. My body knew what to do, va just had to give it the orders. But after Roderick broke my neck, the orders didn't travel anymore." She pushed her head upright again. "It doesn't matter. What was I, when I was alive? I was no use to anyone, least of all myself. I was a pretty doll for my mother to dress up and for men to look at, and then she died and eventually I came here, where there were no men to look at me. And at last, I found a purpose." She smiled up at me. There were white threads at the corners of her mouth and when she spoke, I could see flashes of her tongue, coated in pale wool. I took another step back.

Evil, Roderick had said. But it wasn't evil that I was seeing here, it was *alien,* a monstrous alienness so far removed from what I understood that every fiber of my being screamed to reject it, to run, to get it *away. . . .*

"Dear Alex," she said, a line forming between her eyebrows. "You understand, don't you? You have to understand. You have to help me save van."

"Maddy, I . . ."

"You *have* to."

"I could never help anything that killed you." Which sounded better than the real truth, which was that I wanted

to shoot the thing she had become and then burn the body
and sow the fields with salt.

"You're helping Roderick."

Shame blossomed in my gut. She wasn't wrong.

"The tarn hasn't hurt anyone," she said. "Not deliberately.
Va doesn't feel pain, so how could va understand? Now va
knows better." Another step forward. "It won't hurt now. And
if I hadn't been so weak, the little bit va has to take to feed
wouldn't have mattered."

Denton had Roderick almost to the door now.

"Maddy, are you asking me to let that thing infect me?"

"Not *infect*." She looked offended at the word. "Just give
van a home. Va's like a child, va needs someone to care for
van, and I know you'll protect van and stand up for van, like
you always did for me."

She walked forward and I backpedaled. I had a gun and
fire and I was probably close to a hundred pounds heavier
and still I retreated.

"Alex . . ."

Denton reached out and grabbed the back of my jacket.
He hauled and I scrambled backward and the last I saw of
Madeline was the door slamming in her face.

There were no locks on the outside. I leaned my weight
against the door. "Get something to block it," I said to Denton. Roderick was propped up against the wall, like a drunk
holding up the bar. The doctor bolted down the hallway.

"Alex?" Maddy knocked on the door.

"That's the sound," mumbled Roderick. "That's the sound.

She's still moving. I can hear it from the crypt. Can't you hear it?"

"I hear it," I assured him.

"Alex. Let me out. You have to help me."

The door shook under a blow and actually shoved me forward an inch. I set my feet and braced my back against it. The tarn was far stronger than Madeline had ever been.

"Alex, I'm begging you!"

"It's not her," said Roderick. He was listing sideways but I didn't dare reach out to catch him. "Easton, sir, it's not really her."

"I know," I told him. "I know it isn't."

"Alex, you have to help me save the tarn!"

"Sir . . . I hear her. . . ."

"So do I, Usher."

Blows rained against the door. How was it so *strong*? I imagined Madeline's fragile wrists beating against the wood. Surely the skin would split under such punishment— but perhaps the tarn didn't care. Why would a fungus care about broken flesh? It didn't feel pain, and now, neither did she.

"Alex!"

Tinnitus roared in my ears, drowning out everything. I welcomed it. It didn't last nearly long enough.

"I'm sorry, Maddy," I said. I don't know if she heard me.

"It sounds like her," Roderick said, "but it's not. It's the other thing."

"I know."

Loud scraping noises heralded the arrival of Denton with a long bench. "Here," he said. "This ought to be big enough to brace on the opposite wall."

It was. Barely. The door opened a crack as he shoved it into place and I saw Madeline's blue-black fingers slide around the edge. Bits of hyphae caught in the rough edges of the wood. The bottom of her hand had been hammered raw, dangling gelid bits of flesh and long white threads.

Her hand caught the door and shoved. The bench struck the wall and I heard the groan of wood—but it held.

"Eaaaastonnn . . ." said the voice from behind the door, no longer Maddy's. "Eaaastonn . . . ?"

"Get the servants out," I told Denton. *All one of them, probably.* I shoved my arm under Roderick's and dragged him to his feet. My back screamed at me that I was no longer young and I would pay the price. *Later,* I told it. *Later I can fall apart from the knees on up.*

Roderick sagged against me. "I knew I would have to kill her," he whispered. "I knew it. I never expected you to come here."

"It's all right," I told him. "It's all right."

We got down the stairs somehow. Roderick started to take more of his own weight. My back was grateful, even if he was slow.

"I meant to have Denton visit then leave," he said. "When he saw how sick she looked, no one would be surprised that she had died after." He lifted a shaking hand to his face. "I'm so sorry, Easton. I'm sorry. I had to end that thing."

I nodded. It was unthinkable, but after what I had seen, I no longer questioned his motives. "It's all right, Roderick. I understand." I thumped him on the back as if he were a dog I was seeking to reassure. Oddly, this seemed to soothe him. "It will be all right." Which was a lie, but one we both needed.

Denton had the servants in the courtyard by the time we reached it. There were only two of them, the ubiquitous manservant and a woman that I supposed was the cook. "I sent the stable boy to the inn with my horse," he said, and I nodded.

Roderick stood on his own, swaying. He nodded to the two servants. "Aaron. Mary. It's over. Please go to the village. I'll . . ." He swallowed. "I'll catch up to you when I can."

Mary turned away, expressionless. Aaron lingered. "Sir . . . may I assist you?" He eyed me with cautious distrust, clearly not sure if I was the architect of Usher's condition or his salvation.

"Not this time." Roderick smiled weakly. In the morning light, his skin was a ghastly shade. "Please, go with Mary. So I don't worry."

"Very well, sir." Aaron drew himself up and bowed, then followed the cook down the road and away from the house.

And then it was only Denton and Roderick and me, standing in the courtyard looking up at the cursed house, at the windows gazing down like alien eyes. The tarn flickered with light and woke reflections in the glass.

"How long until she gets out, do you think?" asked Denton.

I swallowed, remembering those hammer-like blows against the door. "Not long. If it doesn't just break her body apart trying." And even that might not stop it. Why should it? I scanned the archway that led to the garden, looking for hares.

"It is simple," said Roderick. "The Ushers have allowed this monstrous thing to grow. The last Usher will see that it does not get out." He nodded quietly to himself.

"You can't go alone," I said at once.

"Yes, I can." He gripped my shoulder. "I still hear her," he added. "I can hear her now. She's in there. She isn't dead.

She isn't dead *enough*. And I can hear the thing in the tarn talking back."

"But what if it . . ."

He smiled angelically at me. "Go, Easton. You are the last of my friends, and the best. Do only this for me."

I swallowed. And then I thumped his back one last time and stepped away and Denton and I staggered away from that accursed house, while Roderick Usher went back inside.

We were halfway down the road, still in sight of the manor house, when the first flame reached the roof.

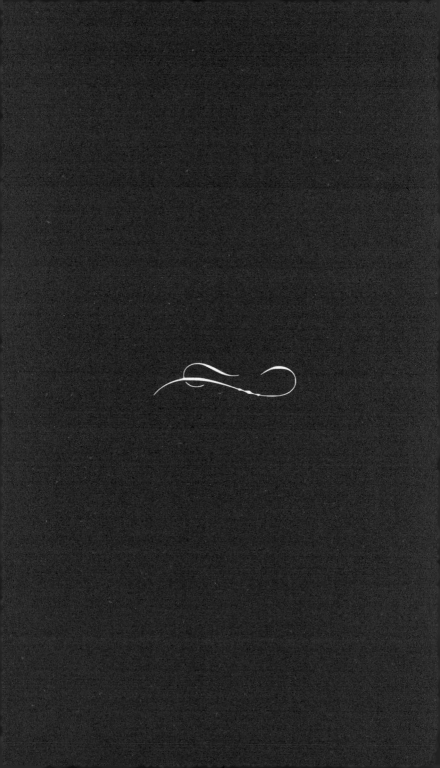

CHAPTER 13

The house burned for two days. Denton and I, dead on our feet, took shifts turning back anyone trying to extinguish it. I must have slept at some point but I honestly have no memory of it.

I listened to the roar of the fire and thought of Roderick saying, "I know exactly where I would place the match."

If the tarn glowed, it was swallowed up by the orange reflections.

At last, when there was clearly no saving the house or anything in it, we went to the village inn. I slept for eighteen hours straight, waking only to drink cold tea and piss it out again. Surely if the water had been boiled for tea, it would be safe. Surely.

When I finally got up, I checked the mirror for any sign of white wool on my tongue. I couldn't see any.

I stumbled down to the common room and found Denton huddled near the fire. "You look like I feel," I told him.

"What a coincidence," he said. "I feel about how you look."

I collapsed into the other chair by the fire. The innkeeper brought me a mug of something. It was hot. That was all I cared about.

We sat there and I drank whatever was in the mug and slowly felt human again. It was not an unmixed blessing. It meant that I could think again, and my thoughts were a horror. Judging by the circles under Denton's eyes, his weren't much better.

"I keep thinking of what it could do," said Denton.

"Take us over, you mean?"

"Not just that." Denton hitched his chair a little closer. "It could move people around. It was learning to talk. Suppose it got better at it. Good enough that no one gave it a second thought. Suppose it spread."

The chill in my bones seemed to radiate outward. "It could go anywhere," I said softly. "Reproduce itself. We'd be at its mercy. Just extensions of it, like the hares."

Denton nodded.

Madeline had said that the tarn meant no harm. Probably neither did rabies. We could not risk humanity on the continued goodwill of an infant monster that could puppet the dead.

I grabbed the poker and stirred up the log, trying to warm myself. "How do we know it's not in us already?"

"I don't know. I think maybe if we don't get a lungful of lake water, we might be all right. It seems to start in the lungs. And Madeline kept going back to the water, maybe to . . . I don't know, maybe so the bit that was in her could talk to the bit in the lake. So maybe if we can destroy what's in the lake somehow . . ." He trailed off. I wondered if there was enough alcohol in the village to cleanse the lake, or, hell, if there was enough alcohol in all of Gallacia.

"How the hell do we destroy a lake?" I asked, as the front door opened.

"Well," said Angus, stamping his feet on the mat, "the wagonload of sulfur we brought seems like a good start."

"Twelve hundred pounds of sulfur!?" I stared from Angus to Miss Potter and back again. "Where did you get—how did you get—?!"

Miss Potter had clearly traveled hard and suffered for it. Her hair was a wild gray tangle and there were immense bags under her eyes. Yet her back was as ramrod straight and her upper lip as stiff as ever, and I was inordinately glad to see both.

Angus looked like Angus. Angus *always* looks like Angus.

"Sulfur," said Miss Potter primly, "is used in the treatment of scab, rust, and a number of other fungal ailments affecting fruit trees. When it became abundantly clear that the authorities were not going to listen to anything we had to say, we stopped by several of the orchards farther down the valley. This is, I am told, the very finest Sicilian sulfur, which is considered superior to the American sort."

"Madam," said Denton, "while normally I might try to defend the honor of my countrymen, at this moment I could kiss both you and your Sicilian sulfur."

"You'll do no such thing," grumbled Angus, "or I'll call you out, Doctor." And Miss Potter actually *blushed*.

"Where's Hob?" I asked, as we went outside.

"Down the valley, standing surety for the return of the wagon and team." Hob was worth three times as much as the pair of draft horses standing in harness, but this was definitely not the time to quibble. The two feather-footed brutes could pull, that was certain. The wagon was piled high with sacks but they did not shirk, not even when the four of us climbed on as well. Angus took up the reins.

To my surprise, Aaron joined us. Angus nodded to him. His face was lean and he looked as weary as the rest of us.

"We're poisoning the lake," said Denton bluntly.

"Oh, aye?"

I closed my eyes while Denton explained about a fungal disease in the lake that caused madness. It was as good an explanation as any, and close to true.

Aaron considered this. "Not surprised, sir. We've known that lake's bad since my grandfather's day."

"You and Mary should take care," said Denton carefully. "It may be spread by drinking the lake water."

I could hear the disbelief in the man's voice. "Nobody drinks *that* water, sir."

Denton paused. "But in the house . . . ?"

"There's a well. A good deep one."

I turned my face away so that no one would see the tears of relief running down it.

Angus and Miss Potter were silent when we reached the ruins. Smoke still rose in thin wisps from the wreckage. The lake was silent, deceptively placid.

We grabbed the bags. The powder struck the surface of the water and for an instant I feared that it would not sink, but then I watched the granules begin to settle, and then they mixed with the water, forming dark swirls that sank deeper into the tarn.

I had turned away to grab a second bag when green radiance flared around us. I saw the glow on the side of the wagon, and the stolid horses shied in sudden alarm. Angus moved to take their heads, murmuring soothing nonsense.

"I daresay that it knows it is under attack," murmured Miss Potter.

"Huh," said Aaron.

The tarn blazed up with sickly light. Pale, gelatinous shapes pulsed in the depths, but it had no power to reach us. I dumped out another bag, then another, my hands caked with the stuff. The tarn could not die fast enough. I even dared to walk over the causeway, among the cracked stones still radiating heat, and throw handfuls as far out into the water as I could reach. *Oh God,* I thought, *will it be enough?*

Slowly, slowly, the light dimmed. I came back for another bag, but Angus stopped me. "We've used it all," he said.

"We need more."

"No, look." Miss Potter pointed. The light was almost gone. As we watched, it pulsed a few more times, and then . . . nothing.

We waited for over an hour, as the sun sank, and there was no change. No glow rose from the water. The jellylike shapes vanished under the darkness and everywhere was a heavy smell of burned things.

"Is it done?" I whispered.

She nodded to me, that fine, stern woman with the heart of a lion. "I believe, Lieutenant, that it is done."

"I'll keep an eye on it," offered Aaron. "If there's any more lights, we'll do what's needful."

"All right," I said. My voice was hoarse and rasping in my ears. "And if you see any hares . . . any animals coming to the water to drink . . . shoot them and burn the bodies. It's important."

"Aye, sir. We will." He reached over and grabbed my fore-arm. I wondered how dreadful I must look that he was trying to comfort me, when his home was a smoking ruin behind us.

And then we drove away and left behind the dead lake and the smoldering timbers of the fallen house of Usher.

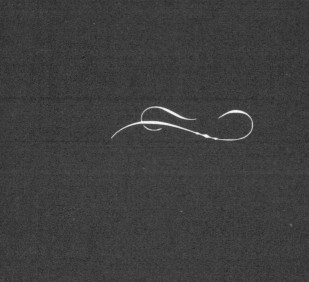

Author's Note

So a while back I happened to reread "The Fall of the House of Usher," as one does, at least when one's horror career involves revisiting classic stories. I'd read it as a child—I was that sort of child—but remembered very little about it.

The first thing I noticed was that Poe is *really* into fungi. He devotes more words to the fungal emanations than he does to Madeline.

The second thing is that it's short. Perhaps because it looms so large in the cultural landscape, I expected it to be much longer. But no, it's short, and while there's a lot to be said about economy of storytelling, I found myself wanting more. I wanted explanations. (I always want explanations.) I wanted to know about Madeline's illness and why Roderick didn't just move and why the narrator didn't bother to check either of them for a pulse before screaming and running from the house.

Well, I couldn't do much about not-checking-for-a-pulse, but it was blindingly obvious to me that Madeline's illness must have something to do with all that fungus everywhere.

I pulled up a blank page and started to write about mushrooms, and all of a sudden Alex Easton was right there on the page, leading kan horse and encountering the fictional aunt of Beatrix Potter (who was herself a noted mycologist). I try not to be too precious about my process, fearing a slippery slope that ends in sighing and swooning and cryptic utterances about the Muse, but the truth is that every now and then a character will simply drop fully formed into my skull, as if they'd simply been waiting for their cue. So it was with Easton.

It's a mixed blessing when that happens. It's a delight for the writer, but such characters tend to warp the whole narrative around themselves. Fortunately Easton was fairly well-behaved—other than strong opinions about Americans—and kindly brought the history of Gallacia trailing in kan wake.

The Ruritanian romance was for many years a genre staple, the story of a small, fictional European monarchy, which really blossomed with *The Prisoner of Zenda*. (Ironically, Easton may actually have read *The Prisoner of Zenda*, since the scientific achievements date *What Moves the Dead* pretty solidly to the 1890s.) But I am much less interested in monarchs than I am in exhausted soldiers and desperate people trapped in falling-down houses, so while the name of Ruravia is a nod to those illustrious forbears, I don't know if this can be said to fit in that grand tradition or if I am merely standing off to the side, giving it a respectful wave.

Well, I went along in fine style for about ten thousand words, learning about Easton's tinnitus and Denton's social missteps and Roderick's decline and sworn soldiers and Gallacian turnip carving, and then I happened to read the magnificent novel *Mexican Gothic,* by Silvia Moreno-Garcia, and thought, "Oh my God, what can I *possibly* do with fungi in a collapsing Gothic house that Moreno-Garcia didn't do ten times better?!" and shoved the whole thing in a virtual drawer and took heavily to the bottle. (Seriously, put down this book and go buy that one. Then pick this one up again, of course, God forbid anyone not finish the Author's Note, but make sure you've put *Mexican Gothic* on your reading list first.)

But.

Well.

As writers say to each other, "Yes, it's been done, but *you* haven't done it yet." And Easton was *right there* and such a wonderful muddle of late-nineteenth-century snobbery and courage and world-weariness and insight, and also my fungus was different, dammit, because, as a Twitter friend once ranted, the problem with many fungus-takes-over-the-brain stories is that the interfaces are deeply incompatible, and I started thinking about how an intelligent fungus would deal with that. What would it be like the first time you realized that these creatures you were puppeting around communicated not by something sensible and straightforward like chemical messages or even photophores but by forcing air over their flaps and modulating the airflow? Light receptors in enclosed balls of fluid, okay, that's not so weird, but everything's wired backward and upside down and you have to figure out how to crack that encoding?

Good God. You'd have to be a genius to work all that out. A genius with a lot of time on your hands.

Of course, the neat trick with fungi is that most of their cells are undifferentiated, so if the majority of cells were effectively brain cells . . . okay, that could give you a really smart mushroom . . . and if you spend a few centuries practicing on the local wildlife . . .

I am, in all honesty, a little sad they had to kill the tarn. I know why they had to do it, but part of me says, "But what if you saved a hare and had a clean room and cultured the fungus in a medium there? Couldn't you learn to communicate? Make friends? It's not malicious; it has no way of knowing that humans really, really hate it when you make dead things walk around. . . ." But with the technology available in the 1890s, and the screaming atavistic horror bit, well. Can't blame anybody, really.

(I must add at this point that in John M. Ford's brilliant Star Trek novel *How Much for Just the Planet?* a character discussing the movie version of "Usher" utters the line, "Sinks into the dark tarn, actually. But there's never a tarn around when you need one." That line was never far from my thoughts.)

Anyway! On to the acknowledgments! Huge thanks to my editors Lindsey Hall and Kelly Lonesome, who heard me say, "I dunno, I have this thing I've been fiddling with, with 'House of Usher' and evil fungi?" and practically climbed down the phone line to pry it from my hands; to my agent, Helen, who had arranged the phone call in question, along with all the other stuff she does so that I can write in peace; to my buddy Shepherd for a beta read and a "It's fine, but also *what is wrong with you!?*"; and to Dr. Catherine Kehl, who helped me brainstorm a lot of things about macroalgae and the nature of the tarn that I wish I'd been able to fit into the book. (There were biofilms on a fungal mat symbiotically overlaying a macroalgae, and the biofilms formed layers and crenelations, and it acted like a brain with electrochemical signaling! It was very cool! But nobody in eighteen ninety whatever would know that! Sigh.)

And of course, as always, to my husband, Kevin, who is the very best at providing encouragement when I have hit that stage of the book where I no longer know if anything is good and am convinced that I have shamed my ancestors forever. Greater love hath no spouse.

T. Kingfisher
July 2020
Pittsboro, NC